The Fountain

KING

Louis Leinweber

ISBN 978-1-0980-1861-0 (paperback)
ISBN 978-1-0980-1862-7 (digital)

Christian Faith Publishing, Inc.
832 Park Avenue
Meadville, PA 16335
www.christianfaithpublishing.com

Printed in the United States of America

Pam Tonsure—owner of Dusty Acres "You
people and your insufferable happiness"
Dill Tonsure—daughter-in-law to Pam
Frank Tonsure—son of Pam
Lemar—male nurse
Tumbleweed Jones
Sally Jones—his daughter
Juanita Cordero—worked for Pam's mom
and dad and is now custodian
Dr. Juan Cordero—son of Juanita (Juancho)
and a doctor who visits Dusty Acres
Chief Thompson—retired navy boatswain's mate chief (BMC)
Beth and Mary—card buddies and lunchies
Billyfred—best friend
Stacy Carbahal—receptionist
Sue Barker—next-door neighbor
Gwen Sangborne—head of operations for Dusty Acres

CHAPTER 1

Sally opened the mailbox and was surprised to see something from her dad. She was to pick him up in an hour and so had time to sit and read. She fixed a cup of coffee with cream and sat at the dining room table. Inside the envelope was a letter and a leather bookmark that had been used by her mother. She held it tightly as she read.

> Dear Sally,
>
> Change has always been hard for me, so please be patient. I remember you told me we don't have time to "mess around" at the old place and that I was to pack my suitcase and be sure to have my toothbrush and comb. I have those things packed, but there are other things. Things I can't pack. Wonderful things that caught me by surprise in this place. Truth be known, I hate to leave them here and am afraid of what is to come.
>
> I get so involved in trying to imagine a thing that I get lost in the details and can hardly see it, and when I think I do have it figured, the eventuality is never what I pictured. I am not disappointed in the situation once it is here, but I must imagine something or I can't proceed. My imagination is like gasoline, both useful and dangerous.

I can count on one hand the number of times I have gone into a situation blind. The most memorable time was when I married your mom. I had no clue how that was going to turn out. I just began and held on with both hands. It was complicated and confusing and wonderful and stressful. A roller coaster is a good description of marriage. That roller coaster is now rusty and broken. Hard to believe it's been five years since she died, and I know it's time for me to move on. I keep forgetting things and would probably burn the house down with me in it. I know. But I am having a hard time imagining me in a retirement home. Do you remember when we all sang at the retirement home for the old ones? One lady even forgot immediately after we sang and asked, "Aren't you going to sing?" Old folks, I guess I am one now.

I will be waiting for you arrival Tuesday morning, as we agreed.

Yours truly,
Dad

PS: Do we have to leave Spartacus with Sue? I still haven't forgiven her for calling the police the time Spartacus treed her precious cat.

Forgiveness, my dear daddy, is one thing you will have to work on, Sally thought. She chuckled and rolled the letter up placing it in the drawer of her desk. She grabbed the keys and made sure the door was locked.

*****

The sky was up where it should be. The birds were singing their usual songs as the trash truck made its way slowly through the neighborhood of Westfall.

Sue Barker stood on the porch and looked over the banister at her neighbor's house. *Something was finally happening over there*, she thought. "Town crier" was her self-appointed duty since retiring. At last, she found something to keep her busy.

Thomas Edison Jones, whom everyone knew as Tom, was being pushed onto the veranda through the French doors by fits and starts. His body lunged back and forth as the wheels crossed the threshold. He winced as he lunged, looking as if he might tumble head over heels into the forsythia. It looked as if Sally couldn't negotiate the wheelchair, but in the end, she did surprisingly well.

Spartacus was at his side, on a leash. He held the leash loosely and looked over at Sue. He smiled when he saw her on the front porch looking at them, holding her morning coffee.

"Hey, Tom," she called, "is that Sally with you?"

"Yes, Miz Barker," Sally said, "and Sparky too."

"His name is Spartacus," Tom whispered, looking slightly perturbed.

Sue began to saunter over to the veranda, looking closely at the grass to avoid Spartacus's droppings. "Today's the big day, is it?"

"Yes, ma'am," Sally said. "I'm taking Daddy to Dusty Acres."

"He's going to be just fine there. I know the owner, and she is the greatest. I had her for a religion class at college. She is quite bright and articulate, but there is one thing that stands out. She has church-o-phobia. Everyone tries to explain Jesus to her, but it's like talking to a brick wall." Sue looked toward the noisy trash truck thoughtfully. "If someone could just take the trash from her mind like we do houses—might take two bags," she said quietly.

"Sorry, I didn't quite hear that," Sally said.

"Just talking to myself."

"As long as you don't answer yourself. That's what Daddy used to say, right Daddy?"

He slowly turned his head toward Sally as his face turned red.

"Maybe Daddy can help her when he gets there."

"It's certainly none of my business," he said.

Sally took the leash from her father and handed it to Sue. "We really appreciate you looking after Sparky while Daddy gets settled."

"His name is Spartacus!" Tom said. "Oh, never mind."

"He won't be a problem," she said, yet in the back of her mind, she wondered how Spartacus and Kittie would get along. "Do you need anything else?"

"No, we have everything we need," Tom said. "Oh, and thanks for the sticky notes." He held the box in the air with his left hand. "I'm not sure what I will do with five thousand wheat-colored sticky notes."

"You'll think of something," Sally said. "You always do." She pushed him down the sidewalk to the car and put on the brakes.

"Turn me around please, and let me get one last look at the house," Tom said. As he looked at the house, he nodded his head several times as if he were counting off a checklist.

Sue watched as they slowly drove away. Sparky barked and pulled hard at the leash so that she had to use both hands and plant her feet to keep him from dragging her to the car.

CHAPTER 2

Pam Tonsure walked over to her stereo and put on her favorite Beethoven CD. She sat at her desk and looked over the list of things she needed to do. She would have to approve a new washer and dryer for the laundry room. *No more cheap stuff but industrial quality*, she thought. Then there was the matter of the activity coordinator quitting over nothing. And, oh yes, *buy a watch*! There were the usual dietary needs to be seen to and a thousand other things too numerous to list, and she had to remember to pack for her trip to see her niece. As she looked around the room, she glanced at the window and saw a hummingbird desperately attempting to get a drink from an empty feeder just outside. *Ha*, she thought, *that will teach you to be so belligerent.*

She remembered that her father had loved hummingbirds. He would watch them for hours in the evenings as he would write his sermons. Sometimes while meditating, he would look up and make pronouncements as if from on high. Once, he said, "Pam, you are soft in the head. You will have to toughen up to survive in this world" or words to that effect. He struggled to be both Mom and Dad to Pam after her mother died. At the time, Pam was just five years old and was crushed. She would go out with father to the store and would be jealous of kids with loving, patient mothers. There was one thing he told her that she did keep in her mind: "Once you have found the truth, do all in your power to guard it." She remembered that.

In kindergarten, she noticed a truth that she resented. Some kids were treated better than others. It was always the stupid ones. She would make up stories to spread around to belittle, to her mind, the special ones—to "even the playing field" so to speak. She remembered one boy who must have been slightly autistic. He would believe anything! Pam chuckled as she remembered something that she had told him in second grade: "Having children is hereditary. If your parents didn't have any kids, you probably won't either." That had him thinking for months. He told her that he would pray about it, and his confusion would be cleared. She remembered laughing out loud at that. She had little patience with people who had imaginary friends. Father had imaginary friends, and look where it got him. She wondered whatever became of the autistic boy until two weeks ago when he showed up at Dusty Acres.

She started life as Pamela Pomace but now felt as dry as her name suggested. Pam's father told her once that Pomace was the stuff left over after squeezing olives. Her mother's death had squeezed her spirit dry. When she thought of her mother, she remembered it was Mom who cared for her and bought her things—who loved her.

It was in college that she was able to divest herself of the Christian trappings that had bogged her down and kept her from feeling at peace while being indignant toward those she felt were clearly beneath her. Father was out of it by then with an early onset Alzheimer's so he wouldn't be ashamed of her. It was liberating. "Pie in the sky" was bad theology, and she took comfort in the thought that *annihilation awaits us all to rub out the evil*. She married right out of college to a professor she had for comparative religion. His name was William Tonsure. He was confident and well-spoken. He was a brilliant debater and was well-loved at the university. He showed her that all religions were similar and man-made, and that choosing one over the other was either arbitrary or hereditary. For the most part, if your parents were Baptist, you were a Baptist; if your parents were Buddhist, you were a Buddhist. She wished that religion had never been invented. Who was the first to believe that some god had blessed them or had his best interests at heart? There is no evidence for such a god. *A truly loving god would make life better in this world,* she thought. *Surely, my husband would not have died and left me alone in this stupid world if God existed.*

Pam and William Tonsure had one child, Frank. He was nothing like William but was identical in nature to her own father. He wouldn't listen to her warnings and even married the girl with that sour name, Dill.

Pam and William bought Dusty Acres when she retired from her teaching job at the university so they would have something to keep them busy. William died two weeks after they moved in.

She wondered why her father liked hummingbirds. All they do is fight all day—sort of like people. He loved people too, she remembered.

*****

B egins a day, a fountain graced.
Arrive, drink, and nectar taste.

*****

The day she was born was like any other day. The sun shone hot in July, and the grass slowly dried in the heat. No breeze blew to cool the gardener as he bent to pull weeds from the rows of corn he had planted at the back of the yard. Every pop of weed root was accompanied by the rich smell of black soil. It was a modest house for the town of Westfall—built on two acres west of town.

Westfall, Texas was the kind of town that you wouldn't just come across unless you were going there. It wasn't on the road from somewhere to somewhere else but was off the beaten path, a perfect place for the cloister like atmosphere of a university and a perfect place for a Methodist pastor and his wife of two years who were expecting their first child. The gardener looked up suddenly as the screen door slammed shut. Reverend Pomace was obviously agitated as he ran back and forth between the car and house, letting the screen door slam every time. "Jesse!" he shouted to the gardener. "Would you look after things for a bit. The time has come."

"Yes, sir, I will." Jesse had never seen him so agitated before but kind of understood, as he too was a father but had long since relaxed about birthing. He shook his head and watched the commotion with a smile. He thought he would have to tell Juanita about it and observe the *cuarentena* if the reverend wanted. That would mean no chili, ice, bacon, or oranges for forty days. Juanita cooked for the reverend and his wife and now would help look after the baby. The door opened once again, and the reverend and his very pregnant wife waddled to the car. He jumped into the driver's seat then out again and ran around to open the door for his wife and carefully strapped her in.

*****

They arrived at the hospital without incident, and things progressed with the usual groaning. The reverend spoke to the doctor and was allowed into the delivery room. Once, as things grew intense, the reverend leaned in to encourage his wife. She grabbed his face, and he suddenly realized that she had the strength and quite possibly the notion to rip his cheeks off. He was a quick study though and thereafter kept a suitable distance. After the transition, things became more peaceful until at last, mother and baby snuggled in the bed with the rattled father looking on, thinking, *This is too much to take in.* The baby made no noise other than an occasional coo. *Absolute peace*, he thought, watching the baby girl nurse on her mother. "What shall we call her?"

"We talked about this." She looked straight into his eyes.

"Oh, I remember. You said Pamela. Pamela Pomace," he said, trying it on for size. "Yes, I think that will do well. And Sue for a middle name after your mom?"

"O kay," she said. "Pamela Sue Pomace, born July 28, 1950. My precious gift."

CHAPTER 3

Dusty Acres was a cross-shaped building with the drive-through entrance at the foot of the cross. The business office was located here, along with a day room up the hall to the nurses' station at the heart. Three wings went from there—one left, one right, and one straight up to the head of the building where meetings and classes were given. It looked like a school at the drop-off, and this is where Sally neatly pulled up and stopped the car, with plenty of room for her father to get out and sit in his wheelchair. After a brief check with Stacy, they were directed to a room. The room was nice, and the shower was good—large enough for him and his wheelchair. He asked about the food because he was bothered with a wheat allergy. Sally pointed to a menu, which the kitchen staff had placed on his writing desk. One thing he liked about Dusty Acres was the writing desk. He could capture the ideas he had been toying with forever but never seemed to have time to jot down.

Sally brought in the box of personal items Tom had packed and began to place them on his desk. Tom noticed her smile as she looked at the stacks of sticky notes that Sue had given him. She placed them beside the pen set.

"Hey, neighbor," someone said from the open door.

"Hello," Tom said.

"My name is Billyfred Jenkins," said the stranger, and he held out his hand to shake Tom's.

"Thomas Jones," Tom said, "but call me Tom. And this is Sally, my daughter."

"Okay, Tom and Sally." He looked up and made a checkmark in the air with his finger, as if putting their names in an invisible notebook. "Tom, do you play pitch? We have a pitch game every Saturday. We need a fourth."

"You mean horseshoes, like *pitching* horseshoes?"

"Not horseshoes. It's a card game, an old cowboy game."

"Don't know if I've ever played, but we can look up the rules. Right, Sally?"

Tom had been trying to get her to become familiar with his phone and had shown her how to look up things. She took his phone and began to look up the rules for pitch. The rules looked awkward, but if Billyfred was willing to explain, he would play. Another face appeared at Tom's door, and it seemed friendly enough.

"Oh, hi, Gwen," Sally said. "Dad, this is Gwen Sangborne, the head of Dusty Acres."

"Hello, Gwen," Tom said. "My name is—"

"Thomas Edison Jones," Gwen said, cutting him off.

Billyfred's eyes opened wide. "I didn't realize we had a Nobel Prize–winning inventor moving in."

Tom looked at the floor and shook his head slowly and said, "I'm afraid I could never live up to that famous name. And it turns out, he never won the Nobel Prize."

"Welcome to Dusty Acres," Gwen said. "I'm sure the nurses have already checked you in?"

"Not exactly," Sally said. "We got the room number at the front desk. They said they would be by soon."

Gwen disappeared, and two nurses quickly appeared with a clipboard each and began to ask Tom questions.

"Believe me, this is going to take *hours*," Billyfred said. "So I will see you at supper."

The nurses got to the business of getting Tom's prescriptions and dietary requirements organized.

It's a good thing Sally is here, Tom thought. She could remember things he had forgotten about his medications. She also reminded him of the prayer group that Gwen mentioned. They would meet every Monday morning at six to pray for the facility and people in need.

Around five o'clock, after Sally and the nurses had left, Tom rolled his chair to the window and saw a pond maybe a hundred yards or so down the hill. *Beautiful,* he thought, and began to appreciate the beauty of Dusty Acres. He wondered about the name, as it was anything but dusty. This was going to be a big change for Tom. He wasn't sure he liked the lack of privacy and the sudden attention. It seemed everything he did was under scrutiny.

Suppertime arrived, and the residents began to shuffle past his door toward the dining hall. Billyfred knocked on the door and invited Tom to sit with him and his card partners. Tom declined the invitation, as he was still kind of shocked from the move and wasn't sure he would be fit company. He pulled the blanket from the foot of his bed and wrapped it around his shoulders and looked out the window as the sun set. He fell asleep and dreamed of glass birds and pencil erasers.

*****

The next morning, Billyfred again knocked on the door, and Tom rolled over and opened it.

"You gotta come eat breakfast. I know you need coffee."

Tom threw the blanket on the bed and brushed his hair. Billyfred pushed him down the hall, and they were greeted by his card-playing buddies, Mary and Beth.

"Hello, Tom," Mary said. "Billyfred told us you just moved in yesterday."

"That's right," Tom said. "I have found it difficult to manage the house since Emma passed." The conversation went well after the initial discomfort of introductions.

After a little while, Mary said, "It's Beth's birthday, and birthdays are usually ignored around here."

"That is unforgivable," Billyfred said, and led the group in singing "Happy Birthday." "That was so pleasurable that I think Tom should collect everyone's birthday so we can go sing for them."

"It's really not my thing to go poke into everyone's business," Tom said.

"Nonsense," Billyfred replied. The girls nodded in agreement.

So it looked as if Tom had a job. They chatted and talked, and Tom began to relax and looked forward to some alone time after breakfast. So he made his excuses and rolled back to his room and began to write his thoughts in the diary Sally left for him. He remembered that in his dream, the glass birds had swallowed the erasers. *Erasers* and *glass birds?* he wrote. *Sometimes dreams mean things*, he thought. He underlined the words then grabbed one of the sticky notepads and placed it in his pocket. He rolled out the door, humming "Happy Birthday" and began a self-guided tour.

Dusty Acres was a medium-sized facility, about eighty beds and about fifteen are unoccupied. It was laid out in a cross shape. He rolled down the hall and ran into one of the male nurses. He had just stepped into the hall, and besides the scrubs, he carried a stethoscope around his neck and had a black beret on his head.

"Sorry, sir," Tom said.

"That's okay," the man said. "We have tough shins with so many wheelchairs around here. My name is Lemar, and you will be seeing see me around."

"Thanks. By the way, when is your birthday? I am supposed to ask because my breakfast group is going to sing for everyone on their birthday."

"My birthday is December 17. Say, you are going to be busy singing for everyone here."

"It *might* be too much, but I think we can handle it." He wrote down the date on one of the sticky notes and stuck it on the arm of the wheelchair.

"By the way it's l-*e*-m-a-r, not l-a-m-a-r," Lemar said. "It's a family name, my grandfather's last name."

"Okay," Tom said as he immediately scratched through the *a* and replaced it with an *e*. He turned his chair around and began to find others to ask: Betty, January 7; Angel, December 21; and Chief Thompson, April 9. Tom nearly had to pull the chief's teeth to get his birthday because all he wanted to do was talk about his time as boatswain's mate in the navy.

As he asked, he would write a separate sticky note and post it on his chair. At first, he felt silly asking, but the responses were so positive that he continued. He even asked the cafeteria people and nurses. Everyone was glad to answer. He began to write their occupation as well so he wouldn't lose track of where they might be on their birthday.

As he neared the office at the foot of the cross, Gwen looked up from her computer and stepped into the hall. "I am glad to see you settle in so well," Gwen said. "Looks like you are going to be a regular part of the team here. We love team players."

This encouraged Tom so he continued his rounds until he had met everyone, except Pam Tonsure who had gone to Alabama to visit her niece. He would ask upon her return to Dusty Acres.

*****

King of the fountain is the play.
Hide in the shadows; scare them away.

*****

Pam's return didn't take long, as she grew tired of her niece badgering her about the things she had her mind made up about. She was a hands-on administrator and insisted upon notification of any new residents. When Stacy sent the memo introducing Tom, Pam's eyes were drawn to the name. *Thomas Edison Jones*, she thought. *Could this be the same one I knew back in school?* She looked over his bio that the nurses had produced with his entry papers and found he had been a computer programmer. *Autistics* can *be programmers*, she thought. She kept watching for him, and finally, she saw him rolling down the hall with those ridiculous notes sticking out all over his chair. She stepped into the hall and said, "You must be the *new* resident. Welcome to Dusty Acres, young man." She grinned. He just looked confused.

"Thanks," Tom said. "I am glad to be here. Everyone has been so nice that I have taken it upon myself to sing 'Happy Birthday' to everyone on their birthday. So if you would let me know your birth-date, I would gladly write it down on one of these sticky notes, and we will sing to you."

"And what makes you think I want some old man singing to me?" she asked. She looked straight into his eyes aggressively.

He looked confused again. He looked as if he were searching for something to say.

"You sort of look like a tumbleweed with all those notes flap-ping," she said. "I'm going to call you Tumbleweed Jones. What do you think about that?"

He paused for about thirty seconds. "Fair enough. Shall I call you Snapdragon?"

If it is him, he has gotten feisty in his old age, she thought. "Everyone calls me Pam or Mrs. Tonsure."

"Okay, Mrs. Tonsure." He spun his wheelchair around. "Can't pin me down 'cause I'm a tumbleweed," he said as he rolled down the hall.

"Bye-bye, Tumbleweed." She made a condescending hand wave. *Yep, its him*, she thought. *Tumbleweed might visit everyone else on their birthday and sing, but not me.*

She stepped back into her room and reached over to her desk to pick up the watch she had purchased on her trip and placed it in her walker basket. She switched off her CD player and began to make her way down to the foot of the cross.

*****

Stacy Carbahal looked out the window at the dreary rain. It had been raining all day, and her socks felt soggy. She tried to keep her mind on the paperwork for Dusty Acres, but the rain reminded her of her mood. She was just getting over a cold and felt just like her socks.

Pam Tonsure, the owner of Dusty Acres, was on her rounds with her squeaky walker. Every time she took a step, it was accompa-nied by a squeak. A metal basket was tied to the front of her walker, which rarely had anything in it; but today, there was a small black box. She always had a scowl on her face; but now, for some unknown reason, she smiled and for a second. Stacy mistook her for someone else. It was the squeak that gave her away. Stacy looked up and said, "Mrs. Tonsure, what brings you down here?"

Pam continued to squeak over toward the desk and grasped the black box with her long fingernails. She held the box up in a trembling hand and said, "I know you like small things, and seeing as you have been *late* lately, I decided to get you this watch. Now see to it you are on time from now on!"

Stacy looked at the box. She was amused that Pam was one of the few people she knew that could give a gift and a slap at the same time, so she was a little confused on how to react. She decided to forgive the slap and accept the gift. She immediately opened it. It was a truly beautiful watch, with a pencil thin brown leather band. She loved that it matched her shoes. Stacy smiled. "Thank you, Pam—I-I mean, Mrs. Tonsure."

"You can thank me by not being late again, young lady." She began to squeak away then turned again. "I love gifts. Don't you?"

"Yes, ma'am, I do." Stacy sat and admired the watch. She looked out the window and remembered other gifts she had been given over the years. She had a loving and patient husband, a beautiful baby girl, and close friends. But the greatest gift was the love of Jesus that caught her by surprise one rainy day years ago. She was sad, knowing that Pam hadn't received that gift.

Offer

Tom sat in the day room, looking out to the pond. He wondered how Spartacus was getting along. He noticed the hummingbirds flying in and out of view around a feeder. He wondered how they flew in the rain. Stacy walked up and said, "Tom."

He looked up. "Yes, ma'am? Please call me Tumbleweed." He realized long ago that if you get a nickname, you may as well embrace it unless it is embarrassing, which the name Tumbleweed was not, he decided.

"Okay, I will. My name is Stacy, and I work for Gwen. She noticed that you might be just the person we are looking for. We checked your background and found that you organized some recreational activities for Boy Scouts one summer and thought you might like to be our new activities coordinator. It would give you something to do, and we could pay you a bit for your services. What do you think?"

Tumbleweed looked around and thought, *This place could use something to get everyone's mind off themselves.* But he realized the headache involved and the endless criticism he would have to endure were a repeat of the Boy Scout fiasco. "No thanks," he said. Tumbleweed noticed a twinkle in her eye when she smiled at his comment.

"Okay," Stacy said, "that is exactly what Gwen thought you would say. So give it some time, think it over, and get back to us."

Tumbleweed sat by the window and thought all afternoon. He remembered that his wife once said that he made Charlie Brown look like Mr. Decisive. The hummingbirds fought and swooped and drank, and by 5 p.m., he noticed that the feeders were running low. He rolled to the cafeteria and asked who filled the feeders. "That would be Juanita," they said. Tumbleweed searched and found Juanita changing the sheets in his room. "Juanita?"

"*Si.* How can I help you, Mr. Tumbleweed?"

News travels fast here, he thought, as he had only recently told Stacy his new name. "I noticed that the hummingbird feeders need some more food."

"Okay, I will fill them, sir. Do you want me to fill them all?"

"Why not?" He noticed that she smiled to herself and, after leaving his room, headed toward the kitchen.

By this time, he had made his decision. He began to think of all the old college professors he could invite to come talk about what they had learned. He could organize fishing trips and outings to museums. He could have preachers of all kinds come and talk—also missionaries, medical doctors, and dietary specialists. He began to wonder what the budget would be, so he called Stacy on the intercom.

"Say, Stacy," Tumbleweed said.

"Yes, Tom—I-I mean Tumbleweed?"

"If I take the job, what will my budget be to get some real talent in here?"

"Well, there is no dedicated budget unless you want to use your pay."

"How much is that?" he asked.

"One hundred dollars a week," she said.

That would pay for one good speaker a week, he thought.

Spartacus

After two weeks, Spartacus began to wonder what he had done wrong to get this kind of punishment. *Everything is upside down. I am drinking with a cat that drools into the water dish. The yard I now have was my toilet, and if that is not weird enough, my old yard is now my toilet. Everything is backwards, and where is Tom? I've had it with this cat. Last night, she scratched my nose, and I had to show her who was boss.*

Sue walked in with a bag. "Come here, Spartacus." *Maybe she has a treat or something.* She pulled something from the bag; it looked like a collar.

Okay, well, this will be okay, he thought. *Whatever tickles your sniffer, lady. It is kind of heavy*, he thought. *There goes that stupid cat again toward my food.* He lunged at the cat, and suddenly, his whole body was paralyzed, twitching uncontrollably. He looked up and whimpered, wagging his tail. *Not sure what happened there. Reminds me of the time we went to the salty big lake. There was a long, skinny fish on the beach, and when my nose just touched it, same thing. But I didn't even touch the stinking cat…Note to self, cat is "no-no" and "bad dog." That is what Sue said anyway.*

Why do they always talk like a baby?

*****

New strength comes but with this thought.
Midday need and having naught.

*****

21

Tumbleweed rolled down the hall, sticky notes in hand, and passed the nurses' station and took a left branch all the way to the end. Pam Tonsure had asked to see him. He wasn't sure what she wanted, but Gwen said he should visit this morning. So off he rolled. He knocked.

"Hello, Tumbleweed," Pam said. "Please come in."

He rolled carefully through the narrow opening and realized she was listening to Beethoven's Symphony no. 7, 2nd movement. He remembered the encounter where she named him Tumbleweed. The atmosphere with the music was ominous. The smell of fresh chocolate cookies filled the air as she handed him a plate with two cookies on it.

"I asked you in so we could get acquainted. I am the owner of Dusty Acres, and as a hands-on kind of person, I like to visit all the new employees to get their take on things."

"No problem, Mrs. Tonsure," he said.

"Just call me Pam," she said. She leaned over and turned the volume to just perceptible.

"Okay, Pam." He considered saying snapdragon but thought better.

"I understand you have joined Gwen's prayer circle," she said.

"I intend to but haven't made a meeting yet."

"Okay, well, there's one thing I have to say about proselytizing around here. No pushing your beliefs, no hard sell. No ganging up. Understand?"

"Yes, ma'am," he said.

"When someone says stop talking, that means stop!"

"Yes, ma'am."

"But if someone asks, then I have no problem with you telling *your* beliefs."

"Yes, ma'am."

"Can't you say anything else?" Pam asked.

"Yes, ma'am," he said. "My mother-in-law once informed me that there were only three things to say to a woman of authority. 'Yes, ma'am,' 'I'm sorry,' and 'You're right.' It worked for her, so I just thought that it would work with you too. It tends to defuse a difficult situation, ma'am." He sounded a bit like Forrest Gump.

"You are really insufferable," Pam said.

"Yes, ma'am," he said.

Pam tapped her foot and looked around. She gripped the rail on her walker and, after a minute, was able to proceed. "Are you going to be the new activities coordinator?" Pam asked.

"I thought I would."

"Well, I believe in a balanced approach. I have a responsibility for the well-being of the residents. Therefore, I want to personally approve *every* idea you come up with, and I will reject anything that I chose. Do you understand?"

"You are the boss."

"After all, if I just let things evolve, they will become higgledy-piggledy chaos. You may be excused." She walked to the window and noticed the hummingbirds fighting over the nectar. "And quit filling these stupid feeders by my window. I am sick of watching them fight all the time. Juanita said you told her to fill them."

"Yes, ma'am," he said and left the room. Tumbleweed smiled as he slowly rolled down the hall toward the day room to wait for lunch. *I just love snapdragons*, he thought.

*****

*****

Pam picked up the phone and rang the front desk. "Yes, Stacy? This is Pam. I wanted to let you know that in my interview with Tumbleweed, I noticed a few things that might indicate early onset Alzheimer's. I would like to have him evaluated by the doctor when he arrives tomorrow."

"Yes mam, I will put it on the schedule"

Pam remembered that her father had not gotten a diagnosis until he was so far gone that he had lost some of her mother's things. Things she wanted. Things she needed to make sense of her life.

Prayer

Monday morning at six came early for Tumbleweed. He rolled out of bed into his wheelchair and looked for something appropriate to wear to a prayer group. In the end, he decided on blue jeans and a pullover shirt. He rolled down the hall to the back of the cafeteria loading dock. Gwen looked up and was surprised to see Tumbleweed rolling in.

"Are you lost?"

"No, I'm here to join the prayer circle, if that is okay."

"Of course it's okay," she said. "Everyone is welcome." She looked around and said, "Tumbleweed, do you know everyone here?"

"Yes, I have met everyone. Hello, Juanita, Angel, Lemar, and Gwen." He held out his hand for a handshake from everyone.

"Fine, then…There are several ground rules we have for our group. First, everything said here stays here. We don't gossip about each other's concerns. Also, no making fun of anyone, God knows it's hard enough without that. Other than that, we talk about how we did as Christians this week and how we can improve. We also mention people for special prayer. If you agree to those rules you are in."

"I am fine." Tumbleweed realized that this reminded him of a prayer group he had attended before.

"Okay, Lemar, I think you were speaking?" Gwen took a sip of coffee and looked at Lemar.

"Well, as I was saying, I need help with the drinking thing. I haven't taken a drink in five years, but it calls to me. It's a strong call, and if it weren't for this group, I would be in a ditch, drunk again. So please, keep me lifted up out of harm's way. That's it for me, but I think Pam needs prayers as she seems to be agitated about something. Since she came back from her niece's house, she hasn't been her usual self. And as the old saying goes, '*When Mama ain't happy, ain't nobody happy.*'"

Gwen said, "I've noticed that as well. She seems to get agitated just before her birthday. I, for one, am pleased that she has sprung for an industrial dryer for the sheets. It could be money that has her concerned. Okay, Tumbleweed, it is now your turn to speak, if you wish. No pressure, though. We all reserve the right to be reticent."

"Please pray for me," Tumbleweed said, "as I take over the activities coordinator. Especially that, as I will be directly supervised by Pam. I don't know how to make her happy. Everything I do or say seems to irritate her. I got snippy with her earlier and called her a snapdragon."

Everyone laughed at that, and Tumbleweed smiled.

"It fits her personality," Gwen said. "That's why we laughed. But we do love her and realize she has been through much. We will pray, especially that she gets to know and love Jesus, as we all do."

"Amen," they all said in unison. And with that, it was over.

As everyone began to go to their duties, Gwen gently grabbed Tumbleweed's arm. "Stay back a moment."

"Okay, what is it?"

"Pam has requested an Alzheimer's evaluation for you today. I don't see why she would request that, as I see no evidence. Nor will the doctor. But you might ask him if you could join the support group anyway, as it would help you with your new duties as activities coordinator. They have great ideas for games and things that keep feeble minds active."

"Okay, I will."

CHAPTER 4

*****

All day long, the fight is on.
Your needs only, grace is gone.

*****

Pam rolled out of bed early around 7 a.m., as she knew the doctor was coming and she had some things to tell him before he made his rounds. She rushed to the dining room and elegantly chewed two pieces of dry toast and coffee. Then she went back to her room. She had told Stacy to let him know to see her first. She had just sat down when he knocked at the door. "Come in."

"Good morning, Pam," said Dr. Cordero.

"Juancho." She smiled, and as always, he smiled back. "Even as a little boy, you had a winning smile. I will never get tired of it."

"Mama said you had something for me today?"

"That's right. We have a new employee, and he is sitting a little high in the saddle. I don't think he has Alzheimer's, but I think a diagnosis would bring him down a peg or two, if you catch my drift."

"Pam, I am a professional. I am licensed, and I have taken an oath to do no harm. I will not give a diagnosis that is untrue. I could be reprimanded or lose my license."

"I am not asking you to give a false diagnosis. Just be vague. Let the poor darling dangle. He has such an imagination that he probably already thinks he has it. I happen to know he has imaginary friends that he talks to."

"Lots of perfectly normal people talk to so-called imaginary friends. I talk to Jesus, who you may consider imaginary but is as real to me as you are."

"I thought you were smarter than that. Didn't they teach you anything in college? Well, I want him evaluated anyway."

"I will administer the test since I do it for all the new residents."

"Let me know how it turns out."

*****

Dr. Juan Cordero left the room and noticed how Beethoven slowly faded out as he turned down the hall to the lounge to meet with all the residents having appointments. Tumbleweed was there, and so was Juanita.

"Hello, Mama," Juan said. He put his hand lovingly on his mom's shoulder.

"Mi hijo," she said, "this is Thomas Jones, who we call Tumble weed."

"Hello, Thomas."

"You can call me Tumbleweed," he said. "It's what Pam wants, and I kind of like it."

"Okay, Tumbleweed, there are a number of tests we normally give to evaluate what might be necessary to make your stay here better. I have a new evaluation software. We give it to all our residents. All you do is sit and answer the questions. Based on your answers, we will have an evaluation."

"I don't think I have dementia, but I heard that Pam has an interest in me having it for some reason."

"Let's just proceed and deal with the consequences later."

Tumbleweed looked up and smiled. "Either way, I want to take the class or support group or whatever, as I am the new activities coordinator. And I heard it might help me come up with ideas for those who do have it."

"Perfect," said the doctor. *I won't have to say anything to Pam because she will assume he has it if he is in the support group.* "Mama is in the group." He turned to Juanita and winked.

"You wish, mi hijo, then you would have someone else to blame *your* bad behavior on."

Juan set his computer up and had Tumbleweed sit as he went through the questions. Tumbleweed's ability meant that he was not a novice with a mouse. He had no trouble negotiating the software. In the end, the test showed some cognitive loss but not due to brain abnormality but standard age decline.

"You are perfectly normal for a man your age. However, I am glad you are going to join the Alzheimer's support group, as I enjoy having company that I can understand."

"When do we meet?" Tumbleweed looked up at the doctor.

"Every Tuesday morning, nine to eleven." He began to look at his sign-in sheet for his next patient, which happened to be Chief Thompson.

"That would be tomorrow. I will see you then." Tumbleweed rolled to the door and nearly ran over the chief as he was stepping through.

"Loose cannon on deck!" said Chief.

"Sorry, sir," Tumbleweed said.

"I *would* say you are three sheets to the wind, but it looks more like eight or nine." He pointed at the sticky notes on Tumbleweed's chair.

Tumbleweed just rolled on through the door and down to the recreation hall for a card game, pondering what the chief meant.

Breakfast revelation

Tuesday breakfast was the usual—scrambled eggs and toast. Tumbleweed looked for the gluten-free toast, but there was none to be had. So he just put eggs and sausage on his plate and sat with the card crew. They were waving at him in line, so he had to sit. He sat with Billyfred, Mary, and Beth for nearly every meal.

Mary scratched butter onto her toast and looked over her glasses at Tumbleweed. "We heard that you failed the cognitive skills test and that you will be in the Alzheimer's support group."

"That's wrong. I simply signed up for the group to get ideas for the activities coordinator job."

"That's not what we heard," said Billyfred. "We have inside information that Pam wants you there. She must have some grudge against you."

"I can't imagine why," said Tumbleweed. "But I have noticed a certain animosity from the day I met her."

"I might know something about it," said Beth. "Maybe...this is *not* the beginning of your relationship. Maybe she is someone you know but can't remember because of your recently diagnosed senility." She winked at Tumbleweed.

Tumbleweed began to search his memory but couldn't think of anything. "I am drawing a blank. Could you enlighten me?"

"Yes, please inform us all," said Mary. She reached for another toast.

"Tumbleweed says that toast will kill you," said Billyfred.

Tumbleweed sat up and said, "I *said* it will kill me. Now, will you please let the dear woman speak?"

Beth took a long sip of coffee, leaned back, and began. "I remember being four years old when my older sister went to Westwood Kindergarten. She came home crying one day because one of her fellow classmates had told her that the teacher thought she was stupid and only gave the stupid kids stars on their conduct sheets. It so happened that my sister got a star every day. The student who told her this was named Suzie Pomace."

Tumbleweed's eyes widened, and he said. "I remember her. She was that preacher's kid, a snake-on-skates. She would lie for fun. She enjoyed confusing me. I was *somewhat* gullible at the time."

Billyfred chuckled and said, "What do you mean *was*?"

"That's not nice," Mary said pointing her butter knife at Billyfred. "Gullibility is a form of guilelessness. It would be better if more of us were guileless like our dear Tumbleweed."

Tumbleweed looked around the table and said, "Was she a friend of Pam or something?"

"This is the best part," Beth said. "She and Pam are one and the same. Pam's full maiden name is Pamela Sue Pomace, now *lovingly* known as Pam Tonsure. Look in her room at her wedding picture. She has it framed like it's a piece of art or something"

Tumbleweed sat back and looked up, "That explains a lot. I will need time to think this over." He looked at his watch and said, "You people are my dear friends, and I thank God for all of you. But I have to run or be late for my first support group meeting."

Billyfred looked up and asked, "Do you need one of us to go with so you don't get lost?"

The girls chuckled slightly.

"I-I…oh, never mind." *Why do they insist on being like that? I will never figure out people.* He rolled down the hall, dodging the walker crowd.

Support group

Chief Thompson walked down the hall to the top of the cross-shaped building where the Alzheimer's support meetings were held. The room was labeled "Head." He thought it was somehow interesting that they would hold meetings in the Head. This meeting room had three walls, with views to the outside with much sunlight and even had skylights too. On partly cloudy days, the sun would come and go through the skylights, seeming to emphasize the doctor's statements. Sometimes, the chief would get so involved in the sunlight that he would float out the window to the water and sometimes, on cloudy days, back to Vietnam. Today was a clear day, however, and he was eager to get a visit from his wife. He was scanning the room for her and was surprised to see Tumbleweed come rolling in. "Ahoy, mate. Come and sit here so we can commiserate our untimely synaptic demise."

"You have a pretty good vocabulary for a Navy man," Tumbleweed said.

"I did crossword puzzles for years in the Navy and was a champion Scrabble man. I had 'em goin' to the dictionary all the time. They got tired of losing, so I had to start reading to pass the time. That is, when I wasn't telling some swabbie how to repair a rusty rivet or escorting some young ensign for a fan room counselling." The chief smiled as he watched Tumbleweed laugh.

"What is a fan room counselling?"

"That's where we teach the poor saps how not to fall down the ladders. Not many have to be taught more than once. How long have you been aboard Tumbleweed?"

"I've been here only two weeks. How about yourself?"

"I can't remember. After my time in the Navy, my wife wanted to travel, but I just couldn't. Things were confusing. Then she started talking about someplace called Dusty Acres or something. A retirement home, I think. Have you ever heard of it?"

"I...I think I have. It's in Westfall, Texas, right?"

"That's the one! My wife lives in Westfall. I told her I would *never* go to a retirement home. That's when she came up with the cruise ship idea. Sea travel I can handle, though I wasn't really sure. Civilians and all...but now...well, there's nothing like *this* fine ship, eh?"

Tumbleweed looked away. "She flies out every few days to visit." He noticed that Tumbleweed seemed uneasy and then said, "I really don't know how we can afford for her to fly back and forth to the ship, but she has assured me that we can."

Tumbleweed looked nervous, then said, "I have to run for a minute before the class begins. Would you hold my seat, please?"

"Roger that."

*****

Tumbleweed rolled out the door and down the hall into the day room. He shook his head and saw the doctor walking toward the conference room. He followed and decided he would ask about the chief after class. They entered the room in single file, and the chief signaled the place for Tumbleweed to sit.

"Today, I would like to discuss how we identify people in trouble—oh hello, Gretchen."

A lovely lady around sixty years old stood in the doorway, looking toward the podium. "I think you will find him over there." He pointed all around the room then landed directly on the chief. The chief stood up and pulled a chair out for the lady. She sat beside him and put her arms around his shoulders.

Chief leaned over toward Tumbleweed and whispered in a loud whisper, "Ain't she the prettiest girl you've ever seen?"

"Is this your wife?" Tumbleweed asked. Chief nodded his head. Tumbleweed looked at her and said, "Hello, Mrs. Thompson, I hope you had a nice flight."

"Ah, we're back on the cruise ship, then?" She looked at the chief, who nodded his head. "Where *else* would we be, darling?"

He turned to look at Tumbleweed. "She has a full-time job, or she would be *here* full-time, right, sweetie?"

"That's right. Now let's pay attention to the doctor." She pointed to the podium where the doctor was talking.

"But then sometimes, it appears that the patient is perfectly lucid and coherent and doesn't have any cognitive dissonance. Then without warning, they go way off track and let you know that something is seriously wrong."

That would explain the chief, Tumbleweed thought. *Clear as a bell one minute, then derailed. What an awful disease!*

"I have a handout that shows some writings from former patients who show this tendency. Chief, would you be so kind as to hand one of these to each person here?"

"Roger that. Leave it to the chief to avoid a snafu." He stood and handed out the copies.

"Let me draw your attention to the first page, where a former patient drew a clock nicely, showing 5:30 as requested. But three years later, the clock shows severely disfigured numbers and hands. This can happen with writing as well. If you would look at page 2, here is some writing from a gentleman that is clear in the beginning. But after a few years of notes, he begins to place numbers into the text, apparently at random. This isn't common but clearly makes no sense.

These things should not frighten or alarm you, but you do need to be aware. So when you see this type of thing, you can get them evaluated. Are there any questions?" He looked around the room, and seeing no hands, he said, "See you next week, then." He gathered up the extra handouts and packed them into his briefcase and walked out.

"That was about as boring as an ensign's briefing." Chief was staring at the pages.

"He is a nice young doctor," Gretchen said.

Tumbleweed looked up. "I was here to get ideas for activities to get people's minds working, but he didn't really cover anything I could use."

"Be here next week. and he will cover something. He is always rambling on and on about it. Why are *we* here anyway, Gretchen? We don't know anyone with ol' timers." He continued to stare at the page.

Gretchen looked at Tumbleweed. Tears welled up, and she said, "It can't hurt, and besides, we have to do *something* with all this time we have."

"Tumbleweed! See this page, it looks like one of our old cypher pages in the navy. They would replace letters with numbers sometimes." He stood up, pointing at the page.

Tumbleweed looked at Gretchen and shook his head as if to say he understood her problem. "Nice to meet you, Gretchen. Have a nice flight home."

"She's not leaving yet," said the chief. "After lunch, we always take a stroll on the weather deck and watch the hummingbirds."

"See you in the chow hall, then."

"Lay to the mess." Chief put his arm gently around Gretchen's shoulders, and they walked out.

Mess

Pam liked Tuesday lunches, as she got to sit and discuss old times with Juanita and Juan. She had known them forever. Juanita was there when she was born, and Juan was like a little brother when he came along. It was Taco Tuesday. Pam had seen so many of the residents struggle with crunchy tacos that she suggested they serve soft ones unless one requested specifically. Pam looked over at Tumbleweed and laughed as his taco exploded all over his plate. Why would he order a crunchy taco when he can have a soft one?

"Juan, what was the result on Tumbleweed? Does he have Alzheimer's?" She knew he was born with something wrong, as she remembered his school days.

"No…some cognitive losses, but no more than expected for one his age."

"Really?" She looked over toward his table and wondered how anyone could observe him and not see how much of a dork he was. It was strange, however, that he seemed to have found some friends. *Maybe they pity him*, she thought. She looked again and saw that Tumbleweed was pointing to the handout that Juan presented at the Alzheimer's meeting.

"Juancho, did you give out Daddy's writings as an example?"

"Yes, Pam, like I always do. You said it was okay to use them. I didn't say where they came from, though."

"That's good. And how is the chief? Still onboard a cruise ship?"

"I guess. I didn't ask. He did seem to be attentive once his wife got there. At first, he and Tumbleweed were talking and not paying attention."

She looked over at the chief and noticed that he and Gretchen had finished eating and were headed outside. On the way out, they stopped at Tumbleweed's table, and Chief pointed at the handout.

"What are they saying about Daddy's writing?"

"Who knows?" Juanita said. "Could be anything."

It was irritating to Pam not knowing, so she walked over to Tumbleweed's table. Chief and Gretchen walked away as she approached.

Billyfred stood and said, "Hello, Mrs. Tonsure."

I don't have time for niceties, she thought. So in her nicest voice, she asked, "What were you and the chief commenting on the hand-out about?" She looked at Tumbleweed, but he seemed to be avoiding eye contact. Everyone else was looking directly at her. Billyfred sat back down. "Pip-pip," she said, "I don't have all day."

"Chief has this crazy notion that the writing example with numbers is coded. He said in the navy they had coded messages that looked like these." He pointed at the page.

"You know he has Alzheimer's, right?"

"Yes, ma'am, hence the word crazy." Tumbleweed looked at her.

She wondered if he was being snippy. She just wanted to slap him and wasn't sure why. *Some people just need to be slapped,* she thought. She knew that public slapping would be bad, so she relied on verbal slaps. "When you are done playing detective, come to my office. I have a proposal. I want to bounce off you. I will expect you at two o'clock." She heard a small but audible gasp from Mary and Beth and smiled, knowing that her slap wasn't wasted."

"Yes, ma'am," he said.

Pam turned and waved goodbye to Juan and Juanita and left the room.

Decipher

Tumbleweed rolled outside for some fresh air and noticed the chief and his wife holding hands and looking at the pond. The snapdragons that Tumbleweed had requested were just beginning to bloom, and the hummers loved them. He wondered what Pam could want with him.

He looked again at the handout and thought about what Billyfred had said at lunch. He told Tumbleweed not to discount what the chief had said because the chief was seldom wrong. *How could Billyfred say that?* he wondered. The chief was in a dreamworld. He doesn't know where he is. *Or is he just pretending?* Tumbleweed pulled out his reading glasses and began to look carefully at the writing. All looked normal until

ST8R2D 37 6Y L4CK2R IT CH5RCH IR2 TH37GS 3
WI7T 9I6 T4 HIV2
TH2 C46B371T347 3S 24 67 9

It sort of looked like writing, he thought. *What if the letters are unchanged, and the numbers represent letters? 1T could be either IT or AT. 3S could be IS or AS. 6Y must be MY, so 6 equals m. Also, T4 must be TO, so 4 equals* o. He substituted these in and found

>
> ST8R2D 37 MY LOCK2R IT CH5RCH IR2 TH37GS 3
> WI7T 9IM TO HIV2

Now the fourth word looks like locker, so let's try 2 equals e.

>
> ST8RED 37 MY LOCKER IT CH5RCH IRE TH37GS 3
> WI7T 9IM TO HIVE

The 1 could be i *or* a. *Let's try 1 equals* i.

>
> ST8RED 37 MY LOCKER IT CH5RCH IRE TH37GS 3
> WI7T 9IM TO HIVE

That isn't good, so let's try 1 equals a.

>
> ST8RED 37 MY LOCKER AT CH5RCH ARE TH37GS 3
> WA7T 9AM TO HAVE

CH5RCH looks like church to me, so 5 equals u, he thought. *Also, the 7 could be an* n.

>
> ST8RED 3N MY LOCKER AT CHURCH ARE TH3NGS 3
> WANT 9AM TO HAVE

That 3 by itself could be an a *or an* i. *Since* a *is taken already, it must be an* i. *3 equals* i.

>
> ST8RED IN MY LOCKER AT CHURCH ARE THINGS I
> WANT 9AM TO HAVE

Now if I put them in the second line,

THE COMBINATION IS EO MN 9

Tumbleweed looked at his watch and noticed it was 2 p.m. It's time for Pam's meeting. He gathered his papers into a bunch and stuffed them into his front pocket and rolled down the hall to the end of the left arm of the cross-shaped building.

*****

*****

Tumbleweed knocked on Pam's door. Immediately, it swung open, and Pam smiled a condescending smile. She swept her arm as to invite him into her room.

"Come in, dear Tumbleweed."

"You said you had a proposal for me?" He looked around the room, and he noticed the wedding picture as Beth had said. He rolled toward it.

"Yes, there is an atheist convention in town, and I would like you to invite someone to come talk to the residents."

"I would rather not." He looked at the picture closely. She *was* Susie Pomace! *No wonder she treats me with such disrespect.* He had wondered whatever became of her but never imagined she could go from preacher's kid to atheist?

"I told you I needed to approve all the speakers you arrange to speak. Here is one I give you prior approval for. Any atheist can speak anytime. You don't need to ask."

"Susie, what would your father say?" He observed her face turn red.

She paused and took a breath. "So you figured it out. I wondered how long it would take. I figured I might get away with it for a year or two as slow as you are."

"Didn't you get enough in school? I was the butt of all your jokes."

"I was just kidding. I meant no harm. Surely you knew I was joking."

"You were a terror to me in school, and I never understood why. You *have* calmed down and became subtler in your aggressions so far. But you still enjoy treating me badly. Whatever happened to your faith? We were in confirmation class together."

"Well, Tumbleweed, I have found that life makes more sense, and I feel a lot less guilt knowing there is no God for which, by the way, there is no evidence. Therefore, you should know that you are free to be as belligerent back to me as you like. And, in the end, it makes no difference since death awaits us all."

"I tried that in school. Every time I fought back, the stakes got higher, and I actually feared for my life at one point."

"Pish-tosh, you were never in any danger."

"You and I remember it differently, but in any case, I choose to forgive rather than wait for God to destroy me."

"Do you forgive *me*, Tumbleweed?"

"Yes, Pam, every day."

"Why, since your forgiveness does not change me, you can still remember it, and I can reoffend."

"Yes, I *can* remember now that I know you wish me ill. I can guard myself so as not to be hurt, and the memories can be written over like paper that has been erased. There is a shadow of the mistake after the eraser does its work, but the paper is still intact and can be used again. If you destroy the paper, it can't be used again. Forgiveness makes a better eraser than destruction."

"Your little holier-than-thou attitude is about to—I don't want to forgive what was done to me. But even if I did want to, I wouldn't know what to forgive. The sin against me happened before I was conscious. I have vague memories of abuse that I don't understand, but the terror I felt still haunts me. People whispering here and there about poor Suzie...secrets kept from me. Which is why I hate secrets and secret meetings like your little prayer group."

"You are free to come to the meetings. It is open to all."

"I don't think I would be welcome there with my nonbeliefs. Besides, I've heard all that drivel before."

"I'm sorry, Pam. I will pray for you."

"Don't waste your time. Just remember that atheists are welcome here."

He realized the conversation was over, so he asked, "Why did you switch from Susie to Pam?" Tumbleweed looked up.

"Mother called me Susie, but after she died, Daddy started calling me Pam."

"Okay, Pam, have a good afternoon."

"Bye-bye, Tumbleweed." She waved her condescending wave.

Tumbleweed rolled slowly back to his room and thought about erasers and glass birds.

Juan

Juan awoke with a start and looked at the clock. *Oh no! Late!* he thought. But then, he heard the kids yelling in the living room. *Saturday. Whew.* He got up and showered and went into the kitchen to get some breakfast when the phone rang. He picked up the phone and said, "Dr. Cordero." He listened for a response and recognized the voice of Stacy Carbahal at Dusty Acres.

"Yes, Dr. Cordero, I hate to bother you on Saturday, but Mrs. Mars is having some trouble breathing. She is in room 114, next to the chief. Could you come by and see if there is anything you can do to help her?"

"Okay, I will be there at 10 a.m." He stuck his head into the living room and announced, "I have to go to Dusty Acres for a bit. I can bring back pizza if you want."

"Yeah, for pizza!" they all shouted.

He looked at his beautiful wife sitting on the couch, trying to play a computer game with the kids. *She is such a good mother to our kids*, he thought. "See you later, sweetheart."

She raised one arm without letting go of the controller to wave goodbye.

"*Vaya con Dios*," she said as she looked up into his eyes.

He felt her gaze; it was as if she could touch his soul. Juan looked at his family and realized how blessed he was to "go with God." What a miserable person he would be without her and God. He ate and went out through the garage.

*****

The Studebaker started, and he had a peaceful drive through town. The traffic was light, as it was a Saturday. And soon, he arrived. He walked past the reception and said, "I'm here."

"Room 114," Stacy said.

He hurried down the hall and entered the room. Lemar was there, leaning over Mrs. Mars, listening to her heart with his stethoscope. "How is she doing?"

Lemar turned his head toward the doctor. "She is better now."

"How are you feeling, Mrs. Mars?"

"I've been better, Doctor. But listen, I had a dream about the kids that live in the attic."

The doctor looked at Lemar, knowing that the building had no attic that people could occupy. "What about the kids?"

"Most were happy, but there was one who was scared because she didn't know something."

"What did she not know?" he asked as he took her blood pressure.

"She thought she didn't belong there but had the suitcase anyway. She didn't know where the suitcase came from or who packed it. The other kids told her to open it, but she was scared to."

"*Sounds* like a dream," he said. "Did it disturb you?"

"Only the part about being scared. No one should be frightened when they are traveling to a new place. If they put their trust in God, they won't be."

"So true," he said and noticed that Lemar nodded. Dr. Cordero looked at her chart. "You have a DNR?" he said.

"That's right. I'm ready to go. My bags are packed, and I know who packed them. No need to prolong the inevitable. I will be fine now. Thanks for checking on me."

"Okay then, I will see you next week for your regular checkup." He leaned over to Lemar and said, "Keep me posted." Then toward the bed, he said, "Good afternoon, Mrs. Mars."

She turned to look out the window. "Oh, please tell Mr. Tumbleweed how much I love the snapdragons he planted. The birds just love them."

The doctor nodded and left for the day room. As the doctor turned the corner, he saw Tumbleweed and friends playing cards. He walked into the day room and said, "Excuse me, Tumbleweed, do you know Mrs. Mars?"

"Yes." He looked at the arm of his wheelchair and pulled one rolled up sticky note out and said, "June Mars, eighty-nine years old. Birthday, July 17. Two daughters, both married. Five grandkids, two girls and three boys. Husband died five years ago. I asked her why she was named June when her birthday was in July, and she said that her mother told her July was no name for a girl or a boy either. Her mother also told her that June was her favorite month, and if June hadn't been late, she would have been born in June anyway."

Dr. Cordero sort of lost his train of thought with so much information but remembered in time. "She asked me to thank you for having the snapdragons planted outside her window."

"I'm glad she likes them. They are in honor of Pam."

"How so?" The doctor pulled up a chair as he expected for this to go on for a while.

"Pam reminds me of a snapdragon. I knew her in school, and she was a terror to me."

"So she is a beautiful, fragrant blossom?"

"No, not the flower, the name. Snapdragon. Teeth and flames."

"Ah…well sometimes people have reasons for their bad behaviors. By the way, I take it you didn't realize that the chief had early stage Alzheimer's."

"No, I was shocked. He was perfectly coherent about a lot of things. Then suddenly, he lost me."

The doctor looked around the room and said, "Long-term memory is affected later in the progress of the disease. Things he did yesterday, he will have trouble remembering."

"So he won't remember that the writing you gave us was in code and not caused by delusions?"

"What writing was that?"

"The examples you handed out in the Alzheimer's support group. The chief noticed that it looked like a coded message from his time in the navy, and Billyfred said not to discount things the chief said because he was rarely wrong. But I remembered that Chief didn't even know where he was, so how could he know stuff? But now you say his long-term memory might be okay, and the navy stuff is long-term stuff, and that makes sense because I studied the handout for an hour or so on Tuesday after class. And it began to make sense, and I have decoded most of it."

"What on earth does it say?" He looked at the rest of the table as they sat with rapt attention.

"Something about how there are things he wants to show the church at 9 a.m. and a combination of some kind."

"Could you show me the message sometime?"

"Sure. How about next Tuesday at the support group?"

"Okay then." Dr. Cordero stood and shook everyone's hand then left for the pizza shop. *Old people and their imaginations*, he thought as he shook his head and smiled, *maybe Pam was right about old Tumbleweed.*

Next week, Tuesday

The weekend went rather slowly. Tumbleweed had awakened early and had time to watch the sunrise. He then rolled over to his desk and looked over the coded message but was still unable to figure out the last two symbols. He pulled out the paper and looked again.

ST8RED IN MY LOCKER AT CHURCH ARE THINGS I
WANT 9AM TO HAVE THE COMBINATION IS EO MN 9

The 8 might be an 0, thus making the word STORED. *That would make sense. But that 9 must be just that a 9. So he wants to have the combination by 9 a.m. What could the combination be? Maybe books of the Bible? Ecclesiastes to Obadiah or Matthew to Nehemiah chapter 9?*

He looked up the first verse of chapter 9 in each.

Ecclesiastes 9:1 states, "So I reflected on all this and concluded that the righteous and the wise and what they do are in God's hands, but no one knows whether love or hate awaits them."

Obadiah 9:1 says, "Your warriors, Teman, will be terrified, and everyone in Esau's mountains will be cut down in the slaughter."

Matthew 9:1 tells, "Jesus stepped into a boat, crossed over and came to his own town."

Nehemiah 9:1 shares, "On the twenty-fourth day of the same month, the Israelites gathered together, fasting and wearing sackcloth and putting dust on their heads."

Tumbleweed began to see the futility in trying to decipher the combination. It could be anything. He closed the book and saw that it was breakfast time, so he rolled down the hall. Billyfred had knocked on his door as he went past, and that kind of woke him out of his stupor.

Billyfred smiled as he knocked on Tumbleweed's door. He knew that if he didn't knock, Tumbleweed would lose track of time and would roll out at half past eleven and miss his Alzheimer's support group. As he walked, he knocked on the girls' doors as well so they could have breakfast together. Tumbleweed rolled in late as usual, and the group hailed him, all waving. He had papers sticking out of his shirt pockets. Beth looked over and said, "I wonder what he has been up to now?"

Mary looked at Beth and smiled. "With him, anything is possible."

"I can't wait to hear," Beth said. "He looks frazzled, like he has been up all night."

Tumbleweed got his tray and rolled over to the table. "Hello, gang, what's up this fine morning?"

Billyfred looked at Tumbleweed's tray and said, "What, no pancakes?" He winked at the girls because he knew what Tumbleweed would say.

"I can't have pancakes. They are poison to me!"

"Relax your jets, Tumbleweed. I was just joking. By the way, what have you been working on?"

"That cypher that Dr. Cordero handed out in the Alzheimer's class. I have it figured. Look." He pulled out the paper, showing how he came to decipher it.

Mary looked carefully at the encryption. "Tumbleweed, have you noticed that 1 through 5 are *a, e, i, o, u*? The vowels?"

"No, Mary, I hadn't. What else do you see?

Mary got her purse and pulled out her pencil and prepared to write. "What was 6 again?"

Billyfred was amazed at the cypher and what Tumbleweed had done. "Looks like 6 was an *m*."

Mary said, "And 7?"

"*N*," Tumbleweed said.

"Do you see where I am going?" Mary said, "I can predict the next two without looking."

Beth smiled and said, "Mary, you are so smarty. What are the next two then?"

Mary looked at Tumbleweed and said, "I guess my accountant training is useful for something. Okay, I think 8 is *o*, and 9 is *p*, like the alphabet *m, n, o, p*, 6, 7, 8, 9. Right?"

"I thought 9 was just 9." Tumbleweed looked confused.

Beth said, "Put the *p* where he has the 9."

STORED IN MY LOCKER AT CHURCH ARE THINGS I
WANT PAM TO HAVE THE COMBINATION IS EO MN P

Tumbleweed scratched his head and said, "Well, I guess it meant something to somebody. Thanks for the help."

Billyfred smiled and said, "What are friends for? Besides, we wouldn't want you to get stretch marks by carrying something so big." He really enjoyed the looks of confusion he could engender on Tumbleweeds face. "Hurry along, or you will miss the Alzheimer's class." He suddenly thought of something that would really get Tumbleweed going. "Pip-pip," he said, imitating Pam.

Tumbleweed's chair stopped. He pointed his index finger over his shoulder at Billyfred, as if to say don't ever say that again. Then he smiled and rolled out of the room toward the Head.

Alzheimer's 2

Tumbleweed directed his wheelchair toward the top of the building and saw the chief and his wife arm in arm, strolling slowly down the hall toward the conference room. "Hello, Chief and Gretchen. How was your flight?"

"Ahoy, mate, I don't think I've had the pleasure. I'm Chief Thompson, and this is my wife, who I guess you know already." He held out his hand for a handshake, and Tumbleweed shook his hand.

Tumbleweed looked into his eyes and said, "Yes, Chief, I met her last week." He searched for a sign of remembrance, but when nothing came, he decided to take another tack. "You told me about the cyphers in the navy."

"That's right. I remember…Your name is, uh, Spindlebrush." He smiled.

"Uh, actually it's, Tumbleweed, sir."

"Ah, yes, Tumbleweed." He turned toward Gretchen. "I was sure it was Spindlebrush." He shook his head slightly snapped his fingers and said, "That's right, there was a Spindlebrush on the Bellatrix."

"My flight was good," Gretchen said. "Let's go in and have a seat. Tumbleweed, you can sit with us."

Dr. Cordero arrived and began to open his briefcase. "Chief, would you like to hand out the papers to everyone today?"

"Roger that. Leave it to the chief to avoid a snafu." He stood and handed out the copies.

Tumbleweed sat and thought, *Today is not a good day for the chief. What a miserable thing dementia is.* He watched the chief stare out the window, and he could tell that the chief was miles away.

After class, Chief stood and said, "Lay to the mess."

Tumbleweed began to head that way when Dr. Cordero said, "Tumbleweed, you saw the chief was confused today?"

Tumbleweed turned to face the doctor and said, "I've never witnessed anything quite as heart-wrenching as a crumbling man."

"That is why we need to figure something to stimulate his mind and stave off the tangles." He picked up the papers at the table and packed them into his briefcase.

Tumbleweed looked down and noticed the papers in his pocket. "Oh, Doctor, I have the cypher decoded." He grabbed the papers and rolled them out flat on the desk. He noticed a suspicious grin on the doctor's face.

Dr. Cordero slowly walked over and said, "Okay, show me this encryption, then."

"Well, my friends at breakfast helped me finish it this morning. The original read, ST8R2D 37 6Y L4CK2R IT CH5RCH IR2 TH37GS 3 WI7T 916 T4 HIV2, TH2 C46B371T347 3S 24 67 9. And by substituting *a, e, i, o, u* for 1, 2, 3, 4, 5 and *m, n, o, p* for 6, 7, 8, 9, it turns into STORED IN MY LOCKER AT CHURCH ARE THINGS I WANT PAM TO HAVE, THE COMBINATION IS EO MN P."

Tumbleweed noticed a surprised look on the doctor's face.

"I-I am surprised. First, that it makes sense. And secondly, that you figured it out."

"I hope it means something to someone."

Dr. Cordero asked, "Could I take a picture of it with you? I mean, hold it up and I will take a picture, if that's okay." Tumbleweed held up the paper and smiled and Dr. Cordero snapped away. "Lay to the mess."

"See you there," Tumbleweed said. "Tell Juanita I said hello."

CHAPTER 5

David

Dill Tonsure hung up the phone and considered just what she had agreed to do. She would be substituting for the English teacher at Westfall High for a week. Frank would be happy for her to be getting out of the house, but she wondered if she was strong enough to handle the kids. She only had thirty minutes to worry though, as it was an emergency, and she didn't even have time to change clothes. She grabbed her purse and made sure she had a hairbrush and lipstick. Out the back door she went and into the car. She made her way to the high school in five minutes and checked into the principal's office and got her temporary name tag. She was escorted to the English classroom to find the teacher just walking out.

"Sorry, I have to leave so soon, but my airplane leaves in one hour," said Mrs. Quail.

Dill looked at the kids and waved, "No problem. I was hoping you could tell me what you were working on before you left."

"Sure," she said, grabbing a sheet of paper from the desk. "It's all written here. We are writing poems. We just studied Shakespeare sonnets and some Japanese haiku, but the poems are freestyle. I told them they don't even have to rhyme, but if they do, they get extra credit for them. That should keep you busy for two days. After that, you can assign *Robinson Crusoe* to read, and they can read it in class." She turned toward the class and announced, "Class, this is Mrs. Tonsure, and she will be your teacher until I return. If I hear of any of you giving her any trouble"—she paused, squinted her eyes, and pointed her index finger at the class—"I will pinch your little heads off when I return."

The students giggled.

"I mean it. Now, say good morning to Mrs. Tonsure." She quit the squint and smiled.

In unison, the class said, "Good morning, Mrs. Tonsure!"

Dill smiled and said, "Good morning, class." She then turned to Mrs. Quail. "I think I can handle it from here, and thanks for the introduction."

"I left my phone number in my desk drawer, just in case you need some encouragement this week. And now, I will leave it with you. Good luck." She turned and walked toward the door, then squinted and pointed at the class until she was out of the room.

Dill walked over to the desk and sat down. She dropped her purse on the desk and leaned back, looking over the class. Most of the kids were writing; some were looking out the window, she presumed, for inspiration. One boy held up his hand. "Yes?" she said.

A small boy with glasses and a friendly smile said, "May I come and ask you a question?"

"Of course. Come up." She watched as some of the boys began to imitate his walk from their chairs by hunching their shoulders up and down and snickering. "What can I help you with?"

"Well…I don't really know what to write about…for the poem. Everybody else seems to know somehow, but I can't think."

"First, what is your name?"

"I am David Spaulding."

"Well, David, nice to meet you. What are you interested in? Do you like cars or airplanes or—"

Suddenly noticing her purse, he pointed at it and said, "Look, you have a hummingbird on your purse. Could I write about that? Or would it be stupid?"

She could see that he lacked self-assurance and wanted to give him a hug, like she would with her own kids. But she resisted the temptation. "I love hummingbirds. That would be a great subject."

"I like the way they fight sometimes." He held up his hands and swooped them around. The kids began to snicker.

"Okay, well, let's see if you can put that into words on paper, then." She pointed back to his chair. He walked away dutifully and got out some paper and began to scratch out some words. "Does everyone have a subject to write about?" She looked around and noticed everyone was busily writing, so she sat down. She looked over at David and noticed his head was moving from side to side as he wrote, and his tongue would switch from side to side, opposite the tilt. She smiled but knew somehow that he would be made fun of if anyone saw him. The day went well with little trouble until the last period when the football boys were rowdy. *They will be a challenge*, she thought.

Just Think

Dr. Cordero sat at lunch with Juanita and Pam and couldn't think of anything to say. He was still in shock from what Tumbleweed had shown him. He couldn't tell Pam because there might be nothing there. He decided to confide in Pam's son, Frank, and see if it made any sense to him. Pam went to get another piece of raisin bread toast, leaving Juan and Juanita alone.

"Mama."

"Yes, my son?"

"Pam's father preached at the Methodist Church on 2nd Street, right?"

"Mi hijo, surely you remember having Easter services there before he died. You were at least ten or so. Why do you ask?"

"I have some information that might be of interest to Pam, but I want to ask her son first, in case it's nothing. Please don't tell Pam anything yet."

"Your secret is safe with me." Pam had just returned and apparently heard the word secret.

"I hate secrets—tell me." Pam smiled, but Juan could tell she was serious.

"If I tell you, it will ruin the surprise," he said.

"I hate surprises as well, so tell."

"We were just going over ideas for your birthday party."

"I hate surprise birthday parties. Just make it like all the others."

"Well, I have to go. Goodbye, Mama—Pam." He touched his forehead, as if to salute.

"Goodbye, Juancho," Pam said. Juan's mom waved and placed her left hand on her heart.

*****

"What's for dinner?" Juan shouted. He set his briefcase down and walked toward the kitchen. His son was frying something in a pan.

"We are having tacos," he said.

"Not again…I had them for lunch. Oh well, let me know when they are ready. I have a phone call to make." He walked into the living room and pulled out his cell phone. Frank Tonsure was in his address book.

"Hello?"

"Hello, Frank, it's Juan."

"Dr. Cordero. Is everything okay? With mom?"

"Oh, yes, all is well with her. I called because a new resident at Acres stumbled upon something that might be of interest to you and Pam."

"What would that be?"

"Do you remember that you gave me some of your father's writings to show as early onset Alzheimer's examples?"

"Yes, I remember I just gave you a page or two. What about them."

"This resident who your mom calls Tumbleweed and one of the men with Alzheimer's teamed up and discovered a code in some of the writing."

"Crazy."

"That's for sure, I was a sceptic until I looked at the translation. Frank, they discovered a key that will allow you to translate everything!"

"The page I copied mentioned a locker. Something like in my locker is something Pam needs and the combination is this, then some letters. Something like that."

"Pop had a locker at church, but surely, they would have cleared it out by now. I could call and ask."

"Like I said, it is up to you. I just thought you should know. The key to translate is fairly simple, and I will give it to you if you want."

"Thanks, Juan. I will check it out and call later if I need the key."

*****

"Who was that on the phone?" Dill asked.

"Dr. Cordero." Frank looked at the ceiling, as if trying to remember something.

"Is your mom okay? Her birthday is coming up soon, isn't it?"

"She's fine. He just wanted to tell me that he discovered something about Pop's writings. He may not have been as loopy as we thought."

"I never thought he was loopy. Just sad." Frank smiled at his wife. *She always says the right things*, he thought.

"How was school?"

"Pretty rowdy bunch, especially the seventh and eighth graders."

"I'm sorry." He reached out and put his hand on her shoulder.

"There was one bright spot, though."

"What was that?"

"There was this small kid in tenth grade English class—might be slightly autistic—that wrote a beautiful poem. I was surprised, especially when he told me what he was going to write about."

"I would like to read it sometime."

"Sounds good. I will ask him if I can copy it for you. Supper is getting cold."

She had cooked spaghetti and a small garden salad. Frank looked around the kitchen and was thankful for his life.

The Church

The Methodist Church in Westfall was a small building, seating no more than two hundred at capacity. It sat on a hill on the western edge of town, next to the cemetery. This was convenient for funerals. The old house where Pam grew up was just to the left of the sanctuary and was now used for storage and offices. It was considered too small for a parsonage, so the housing committee agreed to pay the pastor a housing allowance instead of paying for its costly repairs and upkeep.

Frank Tonsure called the number for the church listed on the web page. The phone rang, and the secretary answered. "Hello?"

"Yes, this is Frank Tonsure."

"Hello, Frank." Mrs. Johnson had known Frank since he was born. His grandfather brought him to church on occasions after he retired. "What can I do for you?"

"Well, I found some papers, indicating that Grandpa had a locker or something at the church. Are you aware of such a thing?" He began to fumble for a paper to write on, just in case.

"Funny you should call because we talked about that at the last SPRC meeting. We have lost the locker combination, and I was about to call a locksmith to come open it for us so we could throw out the old papers or whatever. There are six lockers, and we have used all but Pastor Tonsure's. And now, we have a need for it."

"I might have the combination."

"That would be fantastic. Then I wouldn't have to spend money to have it opened."

"I will be right down."

"Okay, I go to lunch in thirty minutes. So could you make it at 2 p.m.?"

"It's a date." Frank folded the cover on his phone and looked up Dr. Cordero. He opened the phone and punched in the numbers, and it began to ring.

"*Hola. Qué puedo hacer para ti.*"

"Hello. Is-is this Dr. Cordero?" Frank looked at the screen to make sure he had punched in the right number.

"Yes, my friend. I thought you were taking Spanish lessons." He chuckled slightly.

"I *have* been taking lessons, but we are still on uh…como…esta…usted?" Frank sounded apologetic.

"No need to apologize. I am happy to see you are interested. What can I do for you?"

"You called the other day and said that Tumbleweed had deciphered the combination of the locker at the Methodist Church."

"That's right. I was astounded. I've been looking at that writing for years and never suspected anything."

"Well the Methodist Church was just about to open it and throw out everything. Since I called in time, I can have it."

"*Fantástico, mi amigo. Obtendré el papel y se lo daré.* I will get the paper and give it to you." Frank heard the phone drop and some rustling of paper, then, "Here it is. STORED IN MY LOCKER AT CHURCH ARE THINGS I WANT PAM TO HAVE; THE COMBINATION IS EO MN P."

"Okay, thanks. If I need anything else, I will call."

"*Estaré en modo de espera.* I will be in standby mode." And he ended the call.

The bilingual nature of the response was somewhat confusing to Frank, but he understood and was thankful—first to Tumbleweed and to the doctor. *Funny how something can be in plain sight but not be seen.* He went to the fridge and made a sandwich.

*****

At two o'clock, Frank arrived at the Methodist Church and found Mrs. Johnson in the office. She looked up when he entered and said, "I was trying to look up the month that Pastor Tonsure retired. I think it was in 1990 or so." She continued to flip papers over and scan them.

"That sounds right. I was in high school. I have the combination. Uh, *e…o…*"

Mrs. Johnson held her hand up and said, "Wait. No sense telling me here. Let's go to the locker, and you can open it." She proceeded through the sanctuary to the back where the old offices were. She stopped just at the door and flipped on the light. It barely helped, as the ceilings were fifteen feet tall and there was only one bulb in a ceramic socket. She pointed to the back wall, where there was a row of rusty old school lockers, which had been donated to the church. "I think his is the first one on the left."

Frank walked around the dusty furniture and looked at his paper, then at the dial. "I have letters, and the locks have numbers. Bummer!" He looked toward Mrs. Johnson.

She looked at her fingernails and said, "I can't help you there. Anyway, I need to type the bulletin." She turned and walked out.

"Thanks." He sat and pulled out his Spanish dictionary and wrote out, "I cannot open it." Then he translated each word. Then he pulled out his phone and called the doctor again.

"Hello, Dr. Cordero speaking."

Frank said, "*Yo no poder abierto eso*. Did you get that?" He heard a slight chuckle on the line.

"What seems to be the problem, Frank?"

"The dial has numbers, and you gave me letters for the combination."

"Let's look at the paper. Well, the original had numbers, and we assumed that they should be translated as well. Maybe they shouldn't have been. The numbers were 24, 67, and 9. Try those and see."

Frank spun the dial clockwise and stopped on 24, then counterclockwise to stop on 67, then clockwise again to 9. He pulled on the locker handle and felt a click. The door swung open, and several pieces of paper fell out. "It's open. Thanks again, Doctor."

"Let me know what is in there."

"Okay, bye." Frank pressed the hang up button and began to survey the contents.

Lemar

"Can you take the trash?" Pam asked. "Someone forgot it yesterday, and it drove me to distraction."

"Yes, ma'am," Lemar said. Even though it wasn't his job, he bent down and picked up the can and pulled the plastic liner and replaced it in one swift move like he had done it a thousand times. Pam looked at her book intently and began to recite something. "What are you studying there?" he asked.

"The Indian way of Nirvana." Pam said. "I have studied all the world religions and have found so many good things in them."

"Yes, ma'am," he said. "Have you ever considered Christianity?"

"Of course," she said. "This culture's myth story."

"Why do you say myth?" he asked. Pam looked up and smiled.

"I perceive you are a Christian," she said. "I wouldn't want to harm your beliefs."

"No offense, ma'am," he said, "but if a gentle college professor could hurt my faith, it would be no faith at all." He turned and left the room to attend to other duties. Pam sat up straight and curled her fingers just so and chanted, "OM," and then, "ASATO MA SAD GAMAYA."

*****

The next day, Lemar arrived to check Pam's heart but found her asleep. As he moved through the room, she woke up and said, "So I could destroy your faith, and you would be okay with that?"

"Sure," he said. "But I have to warn you that if you continue to pray the way you did yesterday, you might be surprised what will happen when you attack *my* faith."

"Sounds like a challenge," she said. "What do you think I was chanting? I just want to know we are on the same page."

"Sure," he said. "I believe you said 'ASATO MA SAD GAMAYA,' which means from delusion, lead me to truth. I googled it. And you will be happy to know that your prayer is being answered."

Pam burst out laughing. Lemar calmly pulled his stethoscope from around his neck and walked over and listened to her heart. He turned to leave, and Pam said, "You think you know something I don't?"

Lemar said, "Your heart sounds good. May I come by sometime after I get off work and visit?"

"I suppose you can," she said.

"Good. Then I will," he said. "Today after 5 p.m."

Pam turned over and began to read from her book.

*****

Lemar arrived promptly at five and was wearing his civilian clothes, not the blue jumper she was used to seeing him in. "If we are going to be friends," he said, "I need to call you something other than Mrs. Tonsure."

"You can call me Pam," she said.

"And you can call me Lemar," he said.

"Well, Lemar, what insightful words of wisdom do you have for me?"

Lemar looked at her face and said, "I know that if you seek the truth, you will find it."

"I know that one," she said. "Matthew 7:7."

"That's right!" he said. "Have you sought the truth?"

"I've been searching my whole life," she said. "I have concluded that we are on our own, a speck of dust in a universe of dust. My body is made of billions of bits of dust from countless exploded stars that accidently came together to form me for a miserable short time. To quote Shakespeare,

> Tomorrow, and tomorrow, and tomorrow,
> Creeps in this petty pace from day to day,
> To the last syllable of recorded time;
> And all our yesterdays have lighted fools
> The way to dusty death. Out, out, brief candle!
> Life's but a walking shadow, a poor player,
> That struts and frets his hour upon the stage,
> And then is heard no more. It is a tale
> Told by an idiot, full of sound and fury,
> Signifying nothing."

Lemar thought for a moment, then said, "You *do* get straight to it, don't you?"

Pam looked at him, and a tear formed in her eye.

"I have been where you are," he said. "I don't know how you got there, but if you tell me about it, I might be able to show you the way out. As I said, I've been in this very situation."

"So you think you are a spiritual spelunker, do you? She said. What do you know about my pain? How could you begin to know what I feel? How I've been abused?"

"Like I said, Pam, I don't know you or your situation, but I know mine. May I tell you about it?"

"I have nothing else going on," Pam said.

Lemar sat down and began. "I was born in East Houston at home, with only my eight brothers and sisters in attendance. Mom worked four jobs to make money to feed us. She was gone most days. My first memory was being slapped by my older brother for 'stealing' food. It was every man for himself at home. Mom said she loved us, and I believe she did. I was glad when school started, and I got some sort of routine going. Most of my teachers gave me hope, but one decided I needed to learn a lesson on what my prospects were for life. She told me every day that I would end up in prison. She said she knew 'my type' and I would one day 'fry in the electric chair.'

By the time I was in high school, these words sounded like a mantra in my mind. I began to believe I was useless, so I may as well look out for number one. Billy, a friend, and I decided to get some money. His mom worked for old man, Kleinschmidt. She told Billy that the old man had 'lots of cash' in a safe. All we had to do was 'break in when the safe was open.' She got paid with cash every Thursday at 5 p.m. She told Billy that Kleinschmidt would go into the closet just before five and get the money for her and the gardener. She listened, and after she was paid, he would go back into the closet and click the safe door shut. We worked out a plan to be there on Thursday. We didn't think things out too well and didn't know Kleinschmidt had a pistol in the safe. Billy and I helped the gardener that day, and when pay time came, we rushed Kleinschmidt. He was fast and grabbed the pistol. I wrestled him for control, and it went off and killed Billy. The gun was in my hand."

"I got twenty years for attempted robbery and manslaughter. The trial was brief, and as the door to my cell shut, I felt I was nothing in a world of nothing. The guards told me I was nothing. I remembered what my teacher had told me. I guess I was in shock for six months or so until one day, my cell mate said something. He said, 'When are you going to wake up and figure out how to get out of here?' I didn't know what he was on about, but I figured that I had not done so well, thinking on my own. So I asked what he meant—"

Suddenly, a knock came at the door. Stacy opened it and said, "Lemar, it's 9 p.m."

"Ah, okay," Lemar said. "May I come again, Pam?"

"Sure," Pam said. "I have to hear the rest of this." She then went to sleep.

Lemar 2

Lemar worked the next day, and when he got to Pam's room, she was asleep. He left her a note.

> Please do me a favor and write a list of things you are sorry for and would change if you could. I will see you this evening at five.

At five, Lemar hadn't arrived. Pam thought that it was typical for Christians to be unreliable. At five-thirty, Lemar arrived. "Sorry, I'm late."

Pam waved her hand and handed him her list. He briefly looked it over and said, "You keep the list."

"Why did I write it?" she asked.

"You will see later," he said. Lemar looked at the ceiling. "I'm trying to remember where I left off."

Pam said, "You were in prison, about to 'wake up.'" She used her fingers to mockingly put quotes around *wake up*.

"Ah, yes," he said. "I remember I was in the situation you described yesterday. A tale told by an idiot signifying nothing. That's good. I've never heard it quite like that before, but it perfectly describes where I was until Parker, my cellie…"

"Cellie?" she said.

"My cellmate," he said. "Two in a room in prison. Parker is now a calm person who never gets rattled. He was a gang member before but quit to become a Christian. He had to get beaten out of the gang. They hurt him, but that day, he changed from anger to peace. I thought he would go back to his old ways. But he didn't, and he is my friend because he saved my life."

"Let me guess," Pam said, "he told you about Jesus, and your life turned around."

"That's right," Lemar said.

"Why does it have to be Jesus?" She asked.

"That was my question too," Lemar said. "There are so many gods out there. Why Jesus? Parker said that Jesus will let himself be known if you seek him."

Pam stood up and grabbed her walker. "I've been looking for God all my life, and he's not to be found!"

Lemar watched her move with agitation and remembered that he too was anxious when Jesus drew close. *As a wild deer fears man, so men fear the approach of Jesus.* "Since you have studied scriptures, I don't have to remind you that Jesus said, "I am the way the truth and the life. No man comes to the Father but by me."

"That would be John 14:6," she said.

"It was this passage that brought me to the door," Lemar said, "and so Parker said the following, 'Dear Jesus, if you are real, please come into my heart and change me.' I said it, and it changed my life."

"I knew better than get into this. I've heard this a thousand times, and I fail to see how it relates to me," Pam said. "Too simple, and who would want a god that plays mind games?" Pam looked at Lemar, and he realized that she had grown tired of the whole process and probably wanted to sleep. "You should leave now!"

Lemar knew better than to press the issue and knew to leave the matter in better hands. "May I see your list again?"

"Why?" she asked.

"So I will know how it changes," he said.

She handed the list to him, and he looked it over carefully. As he suspected, she had written sarcastic anti-Christian things. She wished she had not listened to her father when she was a child and such. He shook his head and handed it back to her. She wadded the paper and threw it into the trash.

"Oh, and by the way," he said, "in the 'tale told by an idiot,' who are you saying the idiot is? Are you trying to say God is the idiot? You are an atheist and yet blame God? You can't have it both ways. If there is no God, then you must be the idiot. I certainly was in my story. I choose every step that lead to chaos. Goodnight, Pam. May God bless you and keep you safe." And with that, he left.

David, May 26

The sun had been up for thirty minutes when David turned the corner to Dusty Acres on his bike. He arrived early so he would have enough time before his mom picked him up for school. He had wanted to have a summer job for a while, but his mom told him she worried that he might not understand the subtleties of orders his bosses might give him and thus fail or be fired. *Thanks for the confidence, Mom.* Dad was silent about it, but he knew his dad approved. He looked over the application and swiftly answered all the questions.

Stacy Carbahal looked over her glasses at the boy who had suddenly shadowed her desk. "Do you need help?"

"Yes, ma'am," he said, "I won't be doing bedpans, will I?"

"No, not for a while," she said. "Just maintenance and trash and vacuuming. Things like that. However, you might have to mop up some disgusting stuff every now and then." She winked at him, and he wasn't sure what to make of that. He handed over the application and turned to leave.

"When can you start?" she asked.

"Today," he said, "after school."

Stacy looked at her watch and said, "Okay then, see you at 4 p.m. Report to Tumbleweed."

He turned to leave, then turned back and grinned. "Where is that?"

"Not where but who. Look there." She pointed down the hall to an old man in a wheelchair with what looked like a hundred yellow strips of paper stuck all over it.

Tumbleweed turned as she pointed and waved. David waved and turned to go to school.

Kitten

The phone alarm sounded like a dog barking. Frank had to walk across the room to shut it off, thus insuring he was awake. He didn't want to miss the once a month visit to his mom at Dusty Acres. He walked over and shook Dill's pillow, and she woke with a snark.

"Oh, its first Saturday again," she said, "and her birthday to boot. I know…We got to get a move on to get there in time."

They showered and changed and made sure the pets had food and water. They drove past the ATM and drew out one hundred and twenty dollars for gas and lunch. The sky was overcast, and a slight drizzle made the wipers necessary. As they drove toward town, Frank noticed something in the middle of his lane. Just before he passed over it, he recognized that it was a kitten—wet, miserable, and lost!

"What was that?" Dill said.

"A kitten," Frank said. "Do you want to pick it up?" He knew full well what the answer was going to be.

"Yes!" said Dill.

Frank turned the car around and put the car in park. He couldn't figure how to turn on the flashers, so he turned on the left blinker and got out. He walked over to the kitten, who had given up on life. There was no fight left in him, so Frank easily picked him up and handed him over to Dill. As it was overcast, it would be okay to leave him in the car while they visited Mom.

They expected this visit to be like every other visit—Mom telling them how they did everything wrong, how Frank was nothing like his father but more like her preacher dad, and how they were a total disappointment to her. But this time, they had a secret, something that would change everything for Pam. He knew now why she was bitter and mean.

"How do we break it to her?" he asked as he turned onto Main Streer.

"You mean the diary?"

"Yes, the diary. I'm glad I didn't read all of it. I guess I will confide with Dr. Cordero and hear what he says."

"That would be good. He might have some wisdom on it. After all, he has known her forever, and Juanita was the reason that she wasn't hurt more than she was." As they drove past Westfall High, a boy on a bicycle pulled onto the sidewalk. "That is the boy who wrote the poem I was telling you about."

"The hummingbirds? He looks younger than I expected." They continued to the hotel to check in.

*****

School dragged by slowly, and there was a test in algebra class that David wasn't really prepared for. He made a B anyway, so he thought that was okay. He stuffed the paper in his backpack as the bell rang. He hopped on his bicycle and arrived at Dusty Acres, with five minutes to spare. He looked around and found Tumbleweed in the dining hall.

"Hello, David," Tumbleweed said. "Is that right?"

"Is what right?" David asked.

"Is your name David?"

"Yes, sir," he said. "I'm David."

"Come help me put this tablecloth on the big table for Pam Tonsure's birthday party."

David helped spread out the cloth and smooth out the wrinkles.

"Oh, I almost forgot." Tumbleweed reached into a side pocket of his wheelchair and handed David a new baseball cap with the Dusty Acres logo. It was a nice hunter green, with a scene of the building amid rolling hills and a weather vane that resembled a sail. "This is so we will know you belong here, and the clients won't have to ask."

"Okay, Mr. Tumbleweed, sir," David said. He placed the cap on his head then took it off and adjusted the strap to fit his large head.

"No need to be formal. Just call me Tumbleweed."

"Okay, Mr. Tumbleweed, sir."

Tumbleweed smiled at the boy and muttered, "No sense in throwing a monkey wrench into your mom's politeness training."

David looked at the old man and said, "Pardon me, sir."

"We have to make rounds now." He reached into his pocket and pulled out a sticky notepad and wrote "PAM'S BIRTHDAY" on one page and "5 PM TODAY, ALL INVITED" on another. He leaned forward and stuck the two notes on the bill of David's cap and said, "Now follow me to the day room."

David followed but so wanted to take the notes off his cap. Still, he thought it was good to be employed, even if it was embarrassing.

Pam got up from her bed and slipped on her house shoes and grabbed her walker and began to squeak down the hall just as Tumbleweed and David came past. "I was just coming to find you Tumbleweed," she said. "Have you posted my party?"

Tumbleweed pointed to David's cap and said, "We were just on the way to—"

"Dear God!" she said. "You have metastasized!"

David shrunk down and looked at the floor.

"Oh, those are my invitations," she said calmly. "Hurry and post them so everyone will have a chance to come. Pip-pip!"

David wondered what she meant by that. He certainly didn't want her to say pip-pip to him. Tumbleweed pulled the notes from David's hat to post them in the day room.

"Aren't you going to sing?" she asked.

"I thought you didn't want some *old man* singing to you," he said.

"Well, I would love to hear David sing. And since you two are joined at the hip, I guess I can bear it." David looked at both hips to make sure he wasn't attached to Tumbleweed somehow and then thought, *Is she going to say pip-pip again?*

Tumbleweed shook his head and said, "Well then, HAPPY BIRTHDAY TO YOU." David could tell he was giving everyone in earshot a chance to help. But in the end, only David sang with him as everyone in the day room was evidently too deaf or disinterested to sing. Anyway, David felt it was a fitting duet. Pam clasped her hands together to the side of her chin with what appeared to be fake joy. Tumbleweed then turned to the day room and announced, "ICE CREAM IN THIRTY MINUTES."

Pam moved past David and whispered, "Welcome to the funny farm."

David looked at Tumbleweed, as if to ask what she meant with a little shrug of his shoulder. But Tumbleweed just smiled.

David pushed his cap back and said, "I thought this was a retirement home, not a funny farm." David then heard Tumbleweed laugh out loud.

*****

Frank and Dill arrived as the cafeteria staff began to set out the ice cream and bowls for the party. Pam arrived in time to cast her disdain on the supplies, but before she could hurt anyone's feelings, Frank hugged her and said, "Happy birthday, Mom."

Pam was apparently disappointed at the turnout.

Frank looked around and wondered about the old man in the wheelchair who had just rolled into the room with a young boy. "What's with the sticky notes?"

Pam spoke up. "Where *are* my manners. Frank and Dill meet Tumbleweed and his trusty sidekick, David. Both new converts to Dusty Acres. As for the sticky notes, you will have to ask the one infested with them."

"Hello, Tumbleweed. So glad you could make it to Mom's birthday party."

"My pleasure. I didn't know Pam had kids."

"Kid, actually. I am the only one. Say, Tumbleweed, what's with the sticky notes?"

"I was given the job to write everyone's birthdate on them, so my card-playing group can remember to sing "Happy Birthday" to them. There are other things I write as well. Notes about children, favorite song, and such. I don't ask, but I write it down if they volunteer the information since I am neither a gossip nor nosy but just want to be friendly."

Frank looked at the rambling insecure old man and wondered, *Could this be the Tumbleweed that Dr. Cordero mentioned? The one that broke the code to Father's notes? How unlikely.* "I understand you broke a code or something?"

"Ah, my fame is spreading. It was really a somewhat simple code, and it was the chief that noticed it. So I'll not take credit for it. He pointed it out at our Alzheimer's support group. He won't remember it now, but he said it looked sort of like the old navy cyphers. And he even pointed out the first word at lunch. Then I spent a couple of hours, and voilà! I had it. That is almost all of it. It took my card-playing buddies to put the finishing touches to it. How did you hear about it? I thought it was just some rambling notes from someone with Alzheimer's."

"That is what we thought too, but sometimes things aren't what they seem. You, my friend, have stumbled onto a mystery that hopefully will lead to the resurrection of a dead heart. I can't tell you about it yet, but I want to thank you." He turned to face Tumbleweed and held out his hand. A tear formed in both his eyes.

Tumbleweed grabbed his hand and shook it slowly, looking into Frank's eyes.

Frank looked over at the table and saw that David was at the table, scarfing down his second bowl of ice cream.

Dill walked over and said, "David, I love the poem you wrote about the hummingbirds."

"I remember. You were the substitute teacher that helped me with the poem."

"Pam, you should see this boy's beautiful poem."

"Sure," Pam said, rolling her eyes slightly. "What is it about?"

"You tell her, David," Dill said.

David put his spoon down and said, "It's about how hummingbirds fight." He held his hands up and began to swoop them back and forth, like he had done in class.

Pam laughed, "You and Tumbleweed are twins, separated by time." She moved over to the table and looked at David and said, "That, my dear child, is *why* I hate hummingbirds. All they do is fight."

"Kind of like looking in the mirror!" David said.

Frank was listening to this conversation and knew that David hit close to home with that one. Pam's face turned red and looked like she was going to physically slap David if he didn't say something. "Mom, did you like the cake?"

"Just a minute, Frank. David was telling me something, and I'm not sure I understood it." Turning to David, she asked, "Exactly what did you mean by that?"

"He's just a kid, Mom," Frank said.

David looked puzzled. "What did I mean by what?"

"The fighting birds are like me looking in the mirror. Look." He pointed at the mirror against the wall by the dining table and lifted his hands in swooping bird–fighting gestures.

Frank suddenly realized he was not trying to point out anything about his mom's character but was innocently looking in the mirror, proud of the way he imitated the hummingbirds. Everyone laughed then, except Pam. Frank looked at his mom, and she had a worried look and a ruffled brow.

After the ice cream, Frank and Dill went back to the hotel. But before they left, Frank said, "Mom, we have been praying for you."

"Typical," she said.

"*What* is typical, Mom?"

"You guys throw a birthday party with no presents then expect me to be happy with your useless prayers."

Frank and Dill just looked at each other sadly. They would continue to pray. Frank felt it *might* be a waste of time, but he knew that feelings weren't always trustworthy, especially that there was new hope: the decoded messages and Grandma's diary.

*****

But now the sun begins to wane.
A change of heart, a gentle reign.

*****

Pam slowly squeaked back to her room and sat on the bed. She felt empty. She decided to go outside. The garden was blooming greatly with snapdragons. *A not so subtle jab from that Tumbleweed,* she thought. She inhaled the fragrance and was surprised at how lovely they smelled. And she began to speak. "Fact is, Tumbleweed understands the game. But David, what is wrong with me? I was ready to fire little David over nothing. Why was I so angry? Maybe it was because he said the truth? Like looking in a mirror! Do I hate the truth? I *do* fight with everyone all day long. Is it because I need to control things? The only thing I got from Dad was his love of truth. The truth is that now, I am tired of fighting, tired of having no one to confide in. William, why did you die?" She began to cry then suddenly sat up and curled her fingers and said, "ASATO MA SAD GAMAYA. From delusion, lead me to truth. Please…someone?"

*****

Diary

A day or two later, Frank sat at his desk and decoded all the notes from his grandfather's locker and opened the diary. The coded notes would not be of interest to his mom. For the most part, they were documented complaints about the church. Grandpa wouldn't want the notes read by the complainers, so they were in code. But the diary, with the beautiful handwriting and messages of love, were not coded. It told the story of a mother who, when she found she was going to die, poured out her love and regrets onto the pages so her daughter, who was too young to read, would later know how much she was loved. It told in detail the mistakes they made and the secrets they kept from Pam or little Suzie as she was called in the diary. On some of the pages, there were drawings that Suzie had evidently drawn—scribbly drawings of horses and things he couldn't identify. Toward the end of the diary, the writing became cruder, he supposed, as Grandmother's pain grew worse. On one of the last pages, Grandmother wrote something that he knew Mom would need to see. He closed the book and wrapped it up in a box, as if it were a present. He put on the label from Tumbleweed, the chief, Mary, Beth, and Billyfred.

Prayer Group 3

Monday arrived, and everyone was present, including Stacy, who had been dropped off early by her husband.

"Hello, Stacy, and welcome to the Monday morning prayer meeting," Lemar said.

"You have been inviting me for months now, and I finally was able to leave the house early enough, as my car is in the shop and Jared had to drop me on his way to work. I mainly wanted to thank Jesus for finding me when I was lost. It was several years ago now. But I can still remember the feeling of being lost, and I cringe when I see it in others.

"I see it in Pam. She is struggling in the dark and crying out. She was in the garden last evening, and she began to talk out loud to no one. I was waiting for Jared to pick me up, so I couldn't help but overhear. I thought about letting her know I was there, but I didn't. I suppose that was a sin, and I need to ask forgiveness for it. But I remembered something that might help Pam. She gave me this watch and said that she likes gifts. Maybe if we bless Pam with a party, she would feel loved. We can call it Boss's Day. I have several ideas for gifts and things to show that we love her, even though she can be tough to deal with at times."

Tumbleweed was nodding his head and said, "I heard her tell Frank that it was a rotten birthday since she didn't get any presents."

Juanita smiled then said, "She doesn't like surprises or secrets. She told us that last week at lunch, but I knew it already since she was a little girl.

"Sometimes..." Lemar said, "sometimes people will avoid the very thing that is sure to help them. They feel the pull but dig in their heels. I know I did."

Gwen looked up and said, "Stacy, when shall we have Boss's Day?"

"Soon, I would think."

"Okay, we will leave the details to you."

"One week from today would give me time to get everyone organized." Stacy looked at her watch and then nodded her head, as if agreeing with herself. "You all bring something nice, and pray for help in the gift you bring. This could be a full-court press so to speak."

Tumbleweed looked up and said, "Let's all bring our gifts here so we can pray over them before the party on Monday."

They all agreed and held hands in prayer to end the meeting.

CHAPTER 6

Sally Jones

Sally drove toward Dusty Acres but stopped off to pick up Sparky. She looked in the bag again to make sure she had the two-sided erasers that Daddy wanted. *Daddy is going to be happy to see Sparky and will be glad to know that he is moving in permanently with me*, she thought. She wondered about the collar as she stepped up to take the leash. "What is with the collar?"

"Sparky got a little rough with Kittie, so I got the collar." She bent down to take off the collar, and Sparky flinched. "It works like a champ if you ever have an unruly dog."

"I will keep that in mind. Thanks for watching Sparky, Sue."

"Bye, and tell your daddy I said hi."

As she drove on to Dusty Acres, she passed a carnival and a gift emporium outside in the school parking lot. *Daddy might like this*, she thought.

As soon as she described the carnival, Daddy was ready to go. "Never know what you might find there," he said.

"I will not take you there with your chair covered in sticky notes!" So they borrowed one from Stacy as they left.

She pushed him around and noticed several craftspeople working, with their hands sculpting cups and plates, and leather workers making billfolds. The smell of cotton candy was everywhere. It was so good to see Sparky and Daddy together. "Why do they call you Tumbleweed at Dusty Acres, Daddy?"

"I suppose it's because of the sticky notes. Pam made up the name, and I guess she wanted to hurt my feelings like she did when I was a kid. Look at these." On a table were several blown glass birds and bottles. He looked closely at them and seemed to be thinking of something. "I need to get someone a gift, and I have a great idea. Here, hold Spartacus for a minute." He disappeared around the dunking booth. When he returned, he held the bag of erasers and a permanent marker. He rolled up to the glassblower and asked him, "Could you blow a bird with something inside?"

The blower looked over at him and said, "It will cost more for a special. What did you have in mind?"

He pointed at one of the display tables and said, "Could you blow a slightly larger hummingbird like one of these with this eraser inside?"

"I think I could. It will take an hour or so."

Daddy took one of the erasers and wrote the word *forgive* on the pink side and *destroy* on the gray side, then handed the eraser to the glassblower. "Please place it in the belly so you can see the words through the side of the bird."

"Will do."

"Sally, let's find something to eat. The smell of popcorn is making me hungry."

Sally looked at her dad with a curious smile. "What are you hungry for?"

"I saw a burger maker with gluten-free buns just over there."

"Now, Daddy, you shouldn't comment on a man's buns like that."

"Does everyone have to give me grief over my grammar?" He smiled.

"You *know* I do," she said. "Payback for when I was a kid."

They sat and ate, and Spartacus ate and was so well-behaved they hardly noticed him. "How about that? Spartacus likes the gluten-free too." After an hour or so, they went back to pick up the bird.

"Say, what is with the words, anyway?" the glassblower asked.

Daddy picked up the bird and looked closely at the words and said, "The way I see it, in this life, you have the right to choose.

Forgiveness or *destruction*. Simple as that." The glassblower scratched his head and looked at Sally, who shrugged her shoulders. He paid the glassblower, and they began to roll back to the car.

"Daddy, who is that bird for?"

"Do you remember when Sue said the owner of Dusty Acres had church-o-phobia?"

"I guess so."

"She just needs a reminder of the consequences of her thinking. It's something we talked about once. It will mean something to her, I hope."

"I thought you said it was none of your business."

"She made it my business."

"How, Daddy?"

"By showing me her pain."

Happy Boss Day

The week dragged by, and everyone thought carefully about gifts for Pam. When Tumbleweed told the chief about Boss's Day in class, he decided to give her his Purple Heart. Gretchen was thinking ahead and told Tumbleweed she would bring another medal to replace the one Chief gave Pam, as she knew he would forget and might accuse Pam of taking it.

Monday arrived, and Tumbleweed rolled out of bed early. He was still excited, as he had gotten a preacher to come talk on Sunday night. It was the first service Dusty Acres had seen in six months. Pam had told the other activities coordinator that no preachers were welcome, and she finally quit over it. Tumbleweed managed to get it past Pam because the sermon was titled "Atheism: True or False." Pam even showed up to listen until the altar call. Then she slowly squeaked out.

Tumbleweed wondered why she stayed so long until she said, "When I close my eyes and listen, that preacher sounds exactly like my father." But that was last night.

He grabbed his present and rolled to the prayer group, where he saw several presents piled up on a table. Gwen was there and was praying over the packages, with tears in her eyes. "I brought one more."

Gwen looked up. "Put it here with the others."

Stacy walked in with a large envelope. "Frank dropped this off this morning." She set it down on the pile and began to pray with Gwen. She looked over at Tumbleweed and said, "Get over here and pray."

"Yes, ma'am," he said as he rolled over and stretched his hands over the pile of packages. Lemar and Juanita arrived and joined the group. They continued for a minute or two when they heard it. It was barely perceptible at first, *s queak-squeak*. Then it became louder, then Pam came in speaking.

"I decided to check out the prayer group this mor—" she stopped in midsentence, mouth open, as she saw the group holding hands, raised over the packages. "Are you all going to sacrifice a chicken or something?"

"No, ma'am," Tumbleweed said. They all dropped their hands. "We were praying over your packages."

"My packages?" She squeaked closer, craning her neck to see.

Gwen cleared her throat. "We planned a surprise Happy Boss Day party. Surprise!"

Everyone then joined and said another disjointed "surprise." It sounded like a question, as they were unsure what the response would be.

"I don't like surprises," she said, "and I—" At this point, everyone joined her in saying "don't like secrets" because they had heard it so many times.

"That's right," she smiled. "When was this party going to happen?"

Gwen spoke up, "Today, right after lunch."

"Okay, since it's not a secret anymore, I will allow it. Stacy, will you schedule a hair-and-nail appointment for me this morning?"

"Yes, ma'am." She immediately left the room.

"Tumbleweed, when David arrives, you and he can put up some signs in the day room, informing everyone to stay late after lunch."

He sat, looking at her, "Pip-pip. I swear you can't move without a pip-pip."

"Yes, ma'am." He rolled for the door slowly.

"Listen to me," she said, shaking her head and looking at the floor, "barking orders like it was my idea."

Gwen walked over and placed her hand on Pam's shoulder. "It's okay, Pam. We are just happy to see you excited."

"You Christians and your insufferable happiness. What am I going to do with you?"

*****

Lunch was spaghetti and meatballs with a salad and breadsticks or nix sticks, as Tumbleweed called them because they were made with wheat. In fact, they had to make a special bowl of rice-spaghetti just for him.

David sat with Tumbleweed and the Ladies, as he called Mary and Beth. They had been kidding David about becoming a regular at the Dusty Acres when he suddenly sat up and said, "Mr. Tumbleweed, sir."

"Yes, David?"

"I hate to spring this on you, but my parents are going on vacation. So next week will be my last week here."

"Okay, David. Well, we certainly will miss you. Right, ladies? If you ever need a letter of recommendation or anything, just come by." Mary and Beth nodded in agreement.

"May I keep the hat?" He grabbed the bill and wiggled it back and forth a little.

Mary said, "The hat is yours. May it guard you and keep you safe now and forever." Beth laughed and patted David on the head then leaned over and kissed him on the cheek. David turned bright red.

They all sat and ate as if it was a regular Monday until desert time. Then Stacy rolled in the podium for announcements. Gwen approached and tested the microphone. "Testing, 1-2-3…is this working? Can anyone hear me?"

"YES!" several shouted.

Then Billyfred added, "Get on with it."

"Okay, well, um…we have decided to have a celebration. I'm sure most of you saw the announcements put up by Tumbleweed and David in the day room. Today, we are celebrating Pam and how thankful we are for her ownership of Dusty Acres."

Sitting next to Tumbleweed at a different table was the chief who leaned over and whispered, "Wow! She owns this ship and Dusty Acres too? She *must* be rich."

Tumbleweed nodded, as he didn't quite know what to say to the chief. Some of the staff pushed in a cart with the gifts and another one with cake and ice cream.

Gwen waved for Pam. "Come up here Pam." The audience began to applaud. "Pam, it is with great admiration and respect that we present you with these gifts to show our appreciation for you."

The crowd began a chant. "Open, open, open."

Pam looked at the packages and picked one up. "Oh, look, one from Stacy."

Stacy quickly opened it and threw the paper on the floor and held up the prize. "Chocolate! I love chocolate. Thank you, Stacy." Stacy smiled.

Pam grabbed another package from the pile. "Oh, one from Tumbleweed. Is it safe to open?" Tumbleweed nodded. She tore open the box and held it up. "Oh, look, a giant hummingbird with a pink-and-grey glob in his stomach. *Tumbleweed*, what in the world? I guess I always knew you were going to give me the bird one day." She immediately set it and the chocolate in her basket and reached for the large envelope. "Here is one from the whole card-playing bunch. Tumbleweed, Mary, Beth, Billyfred, and the chief?"

Tumbleweed looked at the podium because he didn't have any idea what it was.

"How cute. A used diary with a broken clasp. Wait—this looks familiar." She opened it and saw that it was her mother's diary. With a trembling voice, she asked, "Where did you get this, Tumbleweed?"

Tumbleweed said, "I have never seen that book in my life."

"Me neither," said Billyfred.

Pam was looking overwhelmed and sat down. Gwen moved to the microphone and said, "Stacy, would you come help me distribute the cake and ice cream, please. I think the gifts are over with for a while."

Pam stood up, put the diary in her basket, and began to squeak out of the cafeteria. Only David noticed because of the commotion around the cake.

*****

She walked down the hallway and into her room and closed the door and began to read.

> Happy 18th birthday, Suzie, or is it Susan?
> Anyway, I am so happy that your father suggested that I create a diary for you since I won't be around to dispense the wisdom that a budding young girl needs to negotiate the waters of this world. I so wanted to see you grow up, but God had other plans. The cancer is in its final stages the doctors tell me. Don't let my passing be a stumbling block for your faith in Jesus. He loves you, like in the song that we sing every night.
> Do you still sing it?

Tears began to well up in her eyes as she remembered the song and the gentle voice of her mother. *Why didn't I get this diary when I was eighteen? Daddy! How could you forget when it was your idea? How is it that I am holding the diary now? Tumbleweed? Chief? Did they read it? Will they make fun of me? Dare I read on and open this Pandora's box?* She guardedly read the whole story of her young life and the true nature of her mother's love. She then realized that the Pandora's box of memories that she was worried about held nothing but hope.

She closed her eyes, and she began to consider the possibility that Jesus was real. Could it be true? Why so complicated? Why so simple? Stupid and profound! A paradox. She remembered she had once read about C. S. Lewis's conversion experience. On a trip to the zoo, he began the ride in a sidecar attached to his brother's motorcycle, a nonbeliever, and arrived at the zoo, a believer; and as she looked up, sunlight broke through the clouds and through the window and awakened her from a miserable long atheistic sleep. She believed! She looked out the window and saw that the rain had left droplets of water on the window, which now began to trickle down in rivulets, washing the dust from the pane just as tears began to wash the pain from her heart. What an idiot she had been in doubting her mother's love. If she had only gotten this diary when she was supposed to—but her father and his bumbling forgetfulness.

In the end, she forgave her father. After all, his brain was tangled.

Over the next few days, she forgave everyone else too. And then the memories began. One by one, memories of things she had done or said to thwart the delicate faith of her students and friends began to bubble up in her mind. She winced as they played out in vivid detail. *How needlessly cruel I was!* she thought. One by one, she asked God to forgive her, which she felt he did. She felt clean. She remembered that Lemar asked her to make a list and she did—this time, a real list. She didn't write everything down though. Some were too private.

She looked over at the table of gifts that everyone had given her on Boss's Day. So many generous thoughts of love were there, love that she felt was undeserved. She wondered about the Purple Heart and how much it must have meant for the chief to give it away. She then noticed the hummingbird Tumbleweed had given her was turned so that the writing on the erasers was visible. She picked up the hummingbird and read *forgive* on the smooth pink eraser half and *destroy* on the gritty grey half of the eraser. When she saw it in the cafeteria that day, she thought that it might be plastic explosive. Why would she think that of Tumbleweed? She hoped he could forgive her. *Tumbleweed was right. Forgiveness is much better.*

Later, she spoke to Frank, who opened the mystery to her. "How is it possible," he asked, "without divine intervention, for five unlikely people to have untangled the threads of a puzzle that led to the recovery of your diary? I am still amazed. Oh, and by the way, no one read the diary, except me. And I only read the first few pages. Once I determined that private things were there, I quit reading."

"Thank you, Frank. I know this comes late but, I love you! You and Dill have been nothing but patient with me and my mouth. I prayed this morning that God would help me control my tongue. Please forgive me for anything I have said that hurt you."

"I need you to forgive me as well, Mom." They embraced, and then Frank left.

CONCLUSION

David worked late in the evening of his last day. Tumbleweed had a few things he wanted done—things he thought he couldn't get away with but David could. After his shift, David said goodbye to everyone, and Chief Thompson gave him a salute. His mom was waiting at the door, but he had to see Pam.

"I came to see you one last time," David said. "I wanted to bring you that poem I wrote."

"Okay," Pam said.

"Probably not as good as you are used to reading. Tumbleweed told me that you love hummingbirds, but I know better."

"That Tumbleweed!" Pam mumbled then smiled.

"Sorry, ma'am, I didn't hear you," David said. He leaned forward to hear better.

"I said let me see."

"You can read it after I leave since my mom is here to pick me up. I filled the hummingbird feeders outside your windows because Tumbleweed said to. I know you don't like them, but he *is* my boss."

"I dislike the fighting, that is all," Pam said. "One bird takes it upon herself to push everyone away to keep them from drinking when there is plenty for all."

"Yes," he said, "but have you watched just at sunset?"

"No, I guess I haven't," she said.

David left, and Pam read.

Consider the Hummingbird

Begins a day, a fountain graced.
Arrive, drink, and nectar taste.
New strength comes but with this thought.
Midday need and having naught.
King of the fountain is the play.
Hide in the shadows; scare them away.
All day long, the fight is on.
Your needs only, grace is gone.

But now the sun begins to wane.
A change of heart, a gentle reign.
The bold aggressor, Fountain King
Allows them in They form a ring.
Love then rules when all who thirst
No longer scrabble to be first.
But queue up nicely one by one
And drink their fill to the setting sun.

Pam was alone when she read the poem. She turned to look out the window as the sun began to set. Out the window, the fighting took on a different nature. "Look," she said, "the bold one has yielded. She is letting them—" She couldn't speak or understand what was happening to her. For the first time since she was five, she began to hear that voice—the gentle, still, soft voice of the Holy Spirit revealing what she was. She was loved! She was forgiven! She could sing. Now, she was no longer the Fountain King.

ACKNOWLEDGMENTS

First, I would like to thank my wife of forty years who has encouraged me, read the drafts and designed the cover layout. Thank you, Cindy.

Next, I would like to thank my daughters for reading and suggesting edits on the early manuscripts.

A special thanks to Charlie Stancil for his help with Navy Jargon, and to Sarah Huffman for help with Spanish grammar.

Finally, to my Grandma Audrey who wished that hummingbirds wouldn't fight.

ABOUT THE AUTHOR

L ouis Leinweber is a retired civil engineer who has always had a desire to tell stories. He lives on 10 acres in rural Texas with Cindy, his wife of forty years. Together, they raised three daughters, who are the delight of their hearts. His interest in writing began early in life with poetry and short stories. At the University of Texas, he took a creative writing class that inspired him. And now with the encouragement of his wife, he has begun to write in earnest.

CPSIA information can be obtained
at www.ICGtesting.com
Printed in the USA
JSHW010725200220
4330JS00001B/17